MINUTE OF DARKNESS

A NOVELLA

And Eighteen Flash
Fiction Stories

BY

jd daniels

SAVVY PRESS

NEW YORK

ISBN: 978-1939113269
Library of Congress Control Number:
2014959269

Savvy Press – Gawanus Books – Saga SF Publishers

Distributed Worldwide

The author wishes to acknowledge the invaluable assistance and support of the following people: World-renown artist Cheryl A. Fausel, the late Paul Lippman, Michael W. Sinclair, Marjorie Carlson Davis, Claudia Bischoff, Suzanne Kelsey, Marsha Perlman, Jeannette Batko, Sandy Daniels, author and editor Ellen Larson (who welcomed her into the Savvy Press corral) and editor, Betty Ann Tyson. She would also like to thank the editors of the literary online journal, *Doorknobs & BodyPaint* for their inspiration and original publication of the flash fiction stories.

For my loved ones…always

CONTENTS

To everything there is a season, and a time to die; a time to plant, and a time to pluck up that which is planted.

Eccles. 3:1–2, KJV

MINUTE OF DARKNESS
PROLOGUE

After dusk Cass Griffith roamed Ankara, torn about what to do next, anxious because she felt she knew what needed to be done, but fearing she didn't have the strength to do it. She stepped around a couple and turned the corner. Ataturk Boulevard, a street she traveled often on her walks around the city, now looked like a hurricane-ravished sea.

"Dammit," she mumbled, turning around to retrace her steps. But the street and sidewalk she had just come down were also filled with marchers waving signs. She'd been warned more than once to stay away from such gatherings in Turkey. And here she was in the middle of one. Listening to others' warnings wasn't one of her strengths.

Ducking her head, she maneuvered through furious people determined to move forward, looking for the first place where she could get to safety. All around her, the throng shouted. She felt smothered and vulnerable. And just like in the states, even in this mass of thousands, she felt alone.

Coming to Ankara had been a mistake. She'd accomplished nothing. And now this.

"Hey, American, stay put!"

Feeling panic rising, she glanced in the direction of the voice. A Turkish woman with chestnut hair signaled for her to wait and started her way. Sevgi, the person who had just given her the horrible news. Sevgi, the woman who lived in the same apartment building. Sevgi Arslan, the last person Cass wanted to see right now.

But fighting the urge to hurry away, she held her position. She'd experienced a stampede of humanity before—at the end of a soccer game in England when drunken fans became overexcited by victory. Five were killed that day while she had remained in her seat watching the onslaught of screaming people. Fingers clasped into fists, she glanced right to left, waiting.

Sevgi now stood shoulder-to-shoulder with her. She had to raise her voice for Cass to hear. "You shouldn't be here!"

Like Cass, the Turkish woman wore a short wool jacket with large buttons, a black and white hat that looked like a helmet, blue jeans, and flat-heeled boots. Their straight hair reached to their elbows. They were the same height—five-nine. At a quick glance they could have been mistaken for sisters. But Sevgi's skin had a darker, more exotic hue. Her eyes were hazel while Cass's were green. It seemed odd to Cass that it was now in the midst of this madness that she noticed the resemblance. Once it had been another woman who had seemed her twin, even her soul mate.

Sevgi yelled again, but Cass didn't catch the words. She was busy recoiling as an ice chunk dropped near her right foot.

Frowning, Cass looked up. On the second floor, two kids in red and blue pajamas no more than three and six stuck their upper bodies out the window. An adult appeared. The kids vanished and the window was slammed shut causing a pile of snow to fall to the ground. It landed on a large cement flower pot holding a miniature pine tree lit in white lights. The horde around them continued to shout and brandish their fists. A woman in a flowing black robe and matching head gear with only her eyes showing withdrew a pair of scissors from her handbag and snipped the string of lights. Cass wondered if this was an act of defiance against the Christian belief or Western beliefs in general.

Inhaling a large gulp of cold air, Cass faced Sevgi who had just stopped talking to a young man and yelled, "What's this about?"

"Government corruption." Whop. Sevgi rammed against her. "Hey!" Cass glared at the back of another man who was already moving out of sight.

In the next second by the force of the human tidal wave, they were swept like debris down the street. Each surge was a struggle to remain afloat. Cass's heart raced as she battled to stand erect.

Only feet away, tripping over a deep hole near a gutter, Sevgi bent over and gasped, breathing heavily.

Cass sidestepped to make room for two other women in flowered headscarves and long polyester coats holding a placard in Turkish that she couldn't translate. A dark-haired man waving a Turkish flag followed.

"There's over one hundred thousand on the streets in Istanbul. They're marching in every city. Look!" Sevgi pointed in the direction of the park where last week Cass had sat on a snow-dusted bench and fed the swans.

"Shit!" Cass said.

Armored tanks and water cannon trucks, looking like ominous invaders from Afghanistan, rumbled toward them. Suddenly Cass couldn't move. Nothing would make her feet step forward. She was immobile.

Sevgi, apparently understanding Cass's dilemma, grabbed her arm. "Come on, I'll get you out of here."

As Cass was dragged, pushed and shoved the tanks ground to a stop. Soldiers directed their rifles at the sky. Shots rang out. Cass locked eyes with a soldier who was aiming his rifle toward the mob. The roar was deafening, terrifying.

Her body lifted from the pavement and then went down with a thud. Her breath had been knocked out of her, but she wasn't bleeding. At least, she didn't think so.

A young man to Cass's right threw a firebomb. Swiftly, he stepped in her direction, extended his hand and jerked her to her feet before disappearing into the ocean of people. Two men with handkerchiefs over their mouths lit and tossed snake-like strings of fireworks. Others threw stones. Hunkering down, Cass scanned the crowd. Sevgi was no longer in sight.

"Dammit, where are you?"

Fighting for balance, a powerful jet of water blasted the crowd and clouds of acrid tear gas covered everything. Taking the onslaught on the side, Cass moaned, coughed and protected her eyes as she dropped to her knees.

Another shot rang out. In a protective move, she clasped her chest. A man with salt-and-pepper hair toppled over and lay beside her. A scar ran from his hairline to his eyebrow. A mustache covered his upper lip. In the madness of the moment, she was sure it was the carpet merchant she'd been avoiding confronting. Desperate, believing death was near, she reached for his shoulder. "I…I'm so…"

His eyes popped open and in the same instant she realized her mistake. It wasn't Umit.

Grateful that she might have another chance to ask for forgiveness, she helped the stranger to his feet. The man eyed her, backed away and ran.

"My God, I have to…I must…before…"

A rock struck Cass's forehead. Her world went black.

1

Cass

"Unusual weather," the taxi driver mumbled, coughing into his glove. "Won't last long."

Cass scowled and pushed open the door, stepping into a foot of snow. Burying her chin in her wool scarf, she buttoned her jacket, then hurried toward the apartment building as the taxi driver continued his story.

"The poor guy was on his way to Diyarbakir. His mother had called. His father had been shot and his brother was taken away by the military. He was Kurdish. Apparently he waited for the train to start then leaped. Such a shame. He couldn't have been more than eighteen. He was just a kid."

Cass cringed. She had come to Ankara with the intention of making the trip a journey that would prove her a stronger woman than when she had left. She didn't want

1

to be reminded that civil war still raged in eastern Turkey. She gnawed on her lower lip. She didn't like snow or frigid, blinding wind. She'd had enough of blizzards. That's why she'd moved to southern California two years back. Several walkers hurried past, shoulders hunched. Nothing good, she told herself, comes from that position.

Hurrying into the building, Cass flicked snow off a glass evil eye that hung on the wall. The last time she'd seen her friend Justina, she'd been holding a similar one. She averted her eyes.

A black cat rubbed against her leg and purred. Before leaving the states, she'd had to euthanize her eighteen-year-old cat, Pop. He'd been the warm body beside her at night, the first one she spoke to in the morning, the one who knew when she was having trouble coping, or when she was most tempted to just give up in her desire for change.

She bent down. "Hi, there pussins, you hungry?" She stroked the cat's fur. "I'll bring you food later." The cat shot out the door.

With a bag in each hand, she straightened her shoulders and tramped up three flights of steps. She walked through a dimly lit hallway until she stood in front of Apartment 34.

Unlocking the door, she went inside.

The posted photos on the internet hadn't been taken to deceive: Rust-colored sofa. Persian rug. Maple table and chair. A closet-sized bedroom near the front door, one single bed. Refrigerator. Stove. Microwave. Dishes. Pots and pans. Silverware. Towels. Clean bathroom with a Western toilet. Everything she needed to make her stay in Turkey comfortable. Good omens all, she assured herself.

Within minutes she stretched out on the bed and bounced a few times to test the mattress's firmness. She picked up the pillow, squeezed it into position behind her, and frowning, pulled out a dog-eared envelope from a stack of paperwork she'd placed on the nightstand. Sighing, she pulled out the letter mailed several years earlier and began

2

to read aloud:

Dear Cass,

Guess who visits me? You won't believe it. I didn't at first. Remember Hattice, Umit Yilmaz's wife? She's a nice lady and an excellent cook. You should taste her dolma. They're to die for. I don't think her husband knows about the visits. I'm not sure, but it doesn't seem likely. Whenever I mention him, she ducks her head.

Justina

P.S. Remember my guinea pig Ralph? Well, I have another little rodent pet. A rat. Oh, don't curl up your pointed nose. He's a sweetie. I call him Bonzy. He visits me every night, and believe it or not, he eats out of my hand. Life is full of unexpected miracles. Oh, and Hattice brought me a Turkish dictionary. I thought I'd spend the time learning the language. Cass, won't you at least write?

Cass's mouth was dry. Her entire face felt rigid with resolve. Through all those years, she had never written Justina. Now, finally her own person, she had returned to face her.

An eeric chant blew through her head like a distant call to prayer. Lowering her eyelids, she let it skim down her skull, enter her throat, encircle her heart and lungs, then settle in her stomach, creating an all-too-familiar ache that she was determined to bury in Ankara.

3

2

Umit

Umit looked beyond his wife's prone body. The towels hanging on the neighbor's snow-covered balcony whipped back and forth, adding to feeling of angst.

"I'd like to see her again, wouldn't you?" Hattice's hair feathered out over the pillow. The bodice of her white, cotton gown was embroidered with pastel flowers. Her fingers were long and slender.

"Perhaps," he said, "but first, we must find out why she's returned."

"Cass was like a daughter to me."

He looked at her. "To me, as well."

She stroked the hairs on his chest. "Are you feeling well?"

"Yes."

She drew her finger over his shoulder, down his arm. Put her hand over his heart. "Someday we should move."

His eyelids lowered. "Yes...someday."

"We could give up our phone service. No one would bother us. We deserve that."

He pulled her close.

If only that could be.

At dawn Umit Yilmaz rose from the bed and dressed quietly. Before putting on his undershirt, he fastened a bullet-proof vest around his stout chest. Light from the lamp highlighted his thick salt-and-pepper hair, making his white hairs appear more prominent. He put on his leather jacket, tweed wool cap, and black scarf before going out into the harsh weather.

It was a morning of strange, erratic wind and shadow-producing snow. The patchwork cobblestone street seemed alive, pulsing with the footprints of long ago dead travelers. Somehow it disquieted Umit and he focused on the minaret that rose high above the mosque. He had come to Ankara seeking to leave his past life in the civil war–torn east, but this writhing, wrestling city offered him few places to be at peace.

The pavement, coated with ice, crunched as he walked. Thread after thread of whirling snow made it difficult to see. Strolling along the hushed street, he wrapped his scarf around his face, thinking of the American woman who had returned to Turkey after so many years. The woman who had left without a farewell, who had disappointed him and his wife, who would most likely do it again.

A heavy wooden door creaked open and slowly closed as another man stepped onto the street.

Umit smiled as his brother Ali skipped twice to catch up to him.

Other men gathered behind them.

Ali leaned toward Umit. "As you requested," he whispered, "I have men following the Griffith woman."

3

Cass

Cass awakened with a start. Someone in the apartment above had their music too loud. She hated loud music more than she abhorred people talking on their cell phones while they drove. She grimaced and slid off the comforter, went to the window and looked out. It was snowing. Most windows in the other buildings were dark. But one held a burning candle. She smiled.

There'd been a time in her life when her home was often lit by candlelight. It was a time when she was into New Age beliefs.

In Salem she had several spiritual encounter sessions. One woman had led her through a past life regression. She had seen herself with flowing hair wearing a toga, holding a book. She was standing on a hill overlooking the rooftops of an ancient city and a high forbidding wall. On her first trip to Turkey not long after her divorce, she had stood on a hillside and recognized the view immediately. It was one of those déjà vu moments she'd read about, but had never experienced until then. Since that time, she never questioned her Turkish soul-connection. She'd lived here in a past life. Period.

Leaving the window she poured a glass of chardonnay and picked up her pack of American Spirits. She had jetlag and knew she needed more sleep than the catnap she'd just taken. A whisper of a breeze blew through the open window helping to sooth her fretful, restless mood.

Tapping her foot she picked up her cell phone. Before leaving the states, she'd found Justina's phone number. Would she answer the phone? Was the number still in service?

Justina and Cass had been a messed up yin and yang pair, like a hammer and a nail or a screwdriver and a screw. Justina had been the one who planned their travels around Greece and Turkey, who bought the bus tickets, who read the travel books, who led the way on their bike trips. Cass had been the follower; the one so flexible that it was hard to get her to say no about anything.

But that was then. This was now. Or so she hoped.

In the states she hadn't been able to make herself add Justina's number to her contact list. Even now, she did it slowly.

A distant meow reminded her to take food down to the street cat. She pushed "Call". The familiar voice made her eyes widen. She took a deep breath. "Hello. Justina? This is Cass." She caught her lower lip between her teeth.

"Ca…ss?"

Had Justina's voice quivered?

Cass rubbed her neck and ran her fingers through her pillow-frazzled long chestnut hair. "Yes. I, uh, I'm in

Ankara and I'd like to...uh...see you. That is, uh, if you would want to see me."

Neither spoke for several moments. Cass realized she was holding her breath. Sitting on the edge of the bed, she made herself let it out.

"You're in Ankara?" Justina finally asked.

"Yes. Could we meet?"

"Why, I...I suppose so. It's been so long."

"Too long."

"Yes... too... long," Justina said.

"How about Tuesday for lunch?"

"Tuesday...for lunch?"

"If that doesn't work for you, I can meet another time. I'm flexible."

"No, Tuesday would be fine."

Justina set the time. Cass named a place familiar to both of them and they said goodbye. Warily, Cass shook her head, attempting to toss away the electrical jolt that she'd felt at hearing Justina's voice.

A cat on the balcony meowed.

Cass stood, went to the cupboard and rummaged through the contents. "Ah, hah. This will do." She headed for the balcony, but that cat was gone.

Grabbing her coat, she left the apartment.

The dim alley was cluttered with garbage and smelled of rotten fruit. The feline was sprawled out on a stack of damp magazines. The cat had cracks on its lips, though it wasn't very old. Each eye was a different color—one blue, one green. Its hair was long and needed brushing. Its suspicious eyes followed Cass's movement as its tail flipped from one side of the magazine to the other.

Cass set down the metal bowl filled with tuna and stepped back.

Leaning against the building, smoking, going over her conversation with Justina, Cass watched the animal devour the food. Cass's gaze flicked toward the street. From the shadows, a man came around the corner. Facing her, he stopped walking. Her red flag of warning kicked in. Pushing away from the wall, she curved her shoulders and walked slowly toward the apartment entrance.

Footsteps told her he was behind her. Her heart thumped. Snowflakes the size of gardenia blooms whipped and whirled.

Dammit.

When the man passed her, Cass's shoulder muscles relaxed.

Once she would never have gone outside after dark alone. Once she would have run when a man frightened her like this.

But not now. Not after her therapy and martial arts classes.

She snatched a glance over her shoulder.

No one.

Good.

Dropping her cigarette butt in the grate at her feet, she entered the building.

Every day in every way she was getting stronger and stronger, she repeated over and over to herself as she climbed the stairs.

4

Justina

The next day in another part of Ankara, Justina Ismit felt a chill creep across her neck. Maybe, she reflected, this bank was haunted. Perhaps the ghost of her mother had followed her to Turkey. Or was the feeling caused from the knowledge that Cass Griffith, a person who knew her past, was back?   That was most likely the true reason for her growing sense of concern.   But what she could do about it, she had no idea.

Adjusting her shoulders, Justina forced thoughts of Cass away and continued typing. A jet plane's roar shook the windows.

Her desk faced her boss Osman Celik's door. As an American, her husband assured her, she was fortunate to be an administrative secretary to a bank manager in the government city of Ankara. There were so many younger, more attractive women who wanted the job. A jade plant with shiny, stiff leaves filled the right-hand corner of her desk. A telephone/fax machine, a monitor, a keyboard, and a telephone took up much of the remaining space. Mini-blinds divided the glass wall of windows into narrow, parallel lines. Busy fingers of other workers tapped on keyboards, sounding like crickets at a pond.

Justina sat as if balancing a book on her head. Her heels rested flat on the floor. She wore a tweed suit. The back of her head was closely cropped. Stylish, dyed-blonde bangs draped over her left eye. She glanced at the clock. 10 a.m. Standing, she picked up a stack of forms that needed to be signed, tapped her boss's door, and upon hearing his grunt, opened it. Mindful not to interrupt his concentration, she placed the papers on the desk. The current year 1997 was stamped prominently in the upper right-hand corner. She touched the date lightly with her forefinger, wondering where the years had gone.

"Thank you," he said, not raising his head.

Justina gave him time to speak again. He did not. She left the room quietly, careful not to make a loud noise when closing the door, careful not to disturb.

A second airplane shot through the sky as a coworker hurried by, bumping the edge of her chair.

Startled, Justina grabbed a rolling pencil.

"Oh, sorry," the man said.

Justina lifted a hand in a "no problem" gesture, repositioned the pencil, and returned to her work. Out of the corner of her eye, she saw the man share a wink with another coworker. Ever so slightly, she shifted her shoulder.

"Justina, would you bring me a cup of tea?"

Justina's fingers hovered over her keyboard. She looked at him, then at the elderly woman hired to serve the tea. This was Turkey. Everyone knew people were employed to serve tea in offices. The woman was standing right by the cart.

12

"The tea would be sweeter served by you, my dear."

She should tell the man to go to hell. In the past, she would have done so without a thought to consequences. Instead, she pushed her chair back.

Her shoes slid across the floor as she headed for the teacart. Justina again considered ignoring the request, but with her Turkish husband Volkan's repeated instructions in mind, she nodded to the older woman standing near the cart, lifted the silver teapot and swallowed her pride.

It was a small thing, after all.

Volkan negotiated all of the bank's loans. He had also gone to the same university as her boss. The men were fond of each other in spite of their differences of family social position and tastes, as friends who have common college stories to share are fond of each other. Volkan hoped that she would please Celik. By pleasing him and the other workers in the office, she would have a better chance of advancing to a higher paying position, which would, of course, benefit them both. Eventually, with their combined income, they would be able to buy a home and afford to start a family.

Every night, like a coach, he reminded her that she was in a different culture, giving her a pep talk about how she should act. Never meet a man's gaze directly. If a man in the office makes a reasonable request, do it. Men talk. You do not want to be labeled an aggressive American woman. Never voice your opinion. Do not confront. Only socialize with those you believe are going to get ahead. Dress professionally. Never cross your legs. Never leave the office until your day's work is complete.

Never, ever show your tattoo.

And smile. Smile. Smile.

Was it too much for him to ask her to be the woman he thought she should be at work? No. She could do it. At least, that's what she told herself every night before she fell into a fitful sleep. If she could only become the person her

Turkish husband wanted her to be, then everything would be fine.

More than fine.

She picked up a tulip-shaped tea glass and saucer and handed it to her coworker with a bright, false grin.

After her lunch break, Justina left a popular American fast-food café and turned toward the bank. She frowned when she saw two begging gypsy children grab a tourist's leg and hang on as the man attempted to free himself. Lowering her eyes, she quickened her gait at the sight of a deformed beggar extending his box. Shuddered when a man passed, scratching his testicles as he turned his prayer beads in his fingers. Stepped away from three women in colorful headscarves. Crossed the street when a woman covered in a full black *chador* came toward her on the sidewalk. Diverted her eyes from a newspaper where half-naked, buxom women adorned the front page.

Justina yearned for her home in America: the food, summer music performed   in the Common, blossoming cherry and apple trees, beautifully manicured lawns, white, painted, clapboard houses with shutters and flower boxes, graying shingles. That was where her mother had taught her to be a good girl. Being a good girl meant that she must remain with her husband, no matter who else she fell in love with; being a good girl meant that her dreams and desires were not important. Once she had rebelled against the ways of her father and mother, and to what avail?

As the eddying snowflakes landed on the sidewalks and mixed with dirt and soot, they dissolved into a slushy soiled brown. Carefully, she wiped off the soles of her boots on the mat before entering the bank lobby. Once in, she reached into her bag and pulled out a cloth. Lifting her right boot, she wiped off the remaining dirt, repeating the act with the left. She deposited the soiled cloth in a nearby wastebasket and headed for the elevator.

Only three feet away, two female coworkers leaned their heads together as they whispered. Justina stared at the toes of her boots, and feeling the coworkers' gaze, fought hysteria.

She leaned forward, pretending to look for something on the floor. Ignore them. They aren't important. She wrung her hands. The nerve endings at her hairline tingled. Justina's head lowered even farther. Tears dampened the fabric and ruined the crispness of the bow she had tied so carefully that morning. Frantically, she tugged at the damaged fabric, her strangled sobs muffled.

Out of the corner of her eye, she saw the coworkers still watching. She pressed her fingers against her quivering lips.

The elevator doors opened. "Poor dear," she heard as the two women stepped inside. "Let's not say anything." The doors closed, rescuing Justina.

The elevator returned empty. In the protection of its interior, Justina retied her tie, blew her nose, and inhaled deeply to control herself. Looking at the pattern in the ceiling, she wiped the tears from her cheeks with the back of her hand. "Oh, God," she whispered. Then, startled that she had spoken out loud, she sniffed and blew her nose again. The doors whirled open. She rushed toward the ladies room. Without forethought, she entered a stall that did not have a Western toilet. She stared at the well-used porcelain fitted into the floor. A red plastic pitcher sat under a dripping faucet.

Justina dropped her chin to her chest and caught another sob.

5

Umit

In a carpet shop in Ulus, a more traditional, less modern section of Ankara, Umit and Ali sat on short-legged stools at a table playing their nightly game of backgammon. Ali, often the child, clapped his hands in glee as he rolled the die. Umit smiled at his brother's sense of pleasure and joy that he might win the game.

The smell of burning wood fanned through the shop lit only by a table lamp's yellow light bulb. Wool and silk carpets and flat weaves hung on the walls. Others were folded in squares and rectangles and stacked floor-to-ceiling. Textiles draped an antique walnut, four-poster bed. Copper and brass pitchers, bowls, honey pots, camel halters, and soldier's helmets covered all flat surfaces.

Ali slid a disk on the game board before speaking. "Do you think her job interview is a ruse?"

"It's possible. Why would a Turkish housing company want to hire an American contractor? Especially a female. You said she hasn't tried to contact Justina Ismit yet, right?"

"We don't think so, but our men are still checking into it."

Umit made another move, then grinned. "Remember when the four of us went dancing and Justina slapped the owner of the place so hard that his head hit a post?"

They laughed, then sat silently playing their game. But Umit continued to think about Cass. She had stolen his and his wife's hearts, then disappeared. What he had later been told, he had never shared with Hattice.

"We did what we had to do. There was no other choice," Ali said.

Umit, massaging the muscles at the base of his neck, glanced at his brother. She was probably trouble, but still...

As if his brother could read his thoughts, Ali patted him on the knee. "Don't worry. I'll keep her out of danger."

A soft, but persistent knocking stopped their game. Ali hurried away. Soon he reentered with the visitor. Umit rose and smiled. "Ah, Benik, come in."

Umit put his hands on the older man's shoulders and touched his stubbly cheeks with his own. Benik did the same. "You must be frozen. Here, sit by the fire."

Benik accepted the small tea glass Ali delivered on a red and white plastic saucer. Dropping two sugar cubes into the liquid, he stirred it with a tiny spoon. "My cousin from Erzurum called. He's worried about the quality of the housing project beginning there this spring. If the homes don't meet proper standards, his family and others could die in the next earthquake. As you know, he lost his nephew in the Bingol quake, and his uncle died when his house crumpled about him in Bolu."

"Yes, of course..."

17

"You have connections. Your cousin is the foreign minister of Turkey and a member of the Council of Ministers for the Black Sea Economic Corporation. My cousin wants some assurance that quality housing will be built."

Umit leaned forward. "I'll make some calls and inquire. If after this, we have further concerns, we can discuss the next step that needs to be taken."

Benik nodded and stood. "I can ask no more." He put his hand over his heart, bowed then left the shop.

Umit turned to Ali. "Unbelievable. Cass Griffin has an interview to be the contractor for a housing project. Damn."

6

Cass

At 1 p.m. Cass stepped out of the apartment building and under an overcast snow-spitting sky headed for her job interview with the Turkish bank manager. Did she really want to work in Turkey? She wasn't sure. At this point, it really didn't matter. The most important thing was to prove to herself that she was a new woman. What kind of woman she was, was yet to be known. If she got the job offer, she could always turn it down. Or if everything went well, she might take it and enjoy a fun time with Justina. She was hoping for the latter.

They'd been friends once. More than friends really. More like soul sisters. Surely they could be friends again.

Cass hesitated and then nodded at a footless, middle-aged man sitting on a wool blanket on the pavement. On her previous visit, Justina had warned her not to give money to street beggars. Those people were organized. The money went to the top, not to them, Justina had insisted. And under Justina's insistence, Cass had not given them a penny.

Nearby, snow-covered canopies protected yellow, pink, orange, fuchsia-colored flowers, and greenery in buckets. An aroma of roasting lamb curled through the air making Cass feel warm and welcomed. Bending, she spoke to the man and put two bills into the box before continuing on.

The restaurant was easy to find. She'd worked there once as a waitress for three months. A fifty-gallon goldfish tank divided seating from the entrance. She wondered if any of the fish were the same.

As she removed her tan wool jacket and fake fur hat, a man her same height in a business suit walked toward her, extending his hand. "You must be Cass Griffith. Welcome to Ankara."

"And you're Timur Sahin." In one glance she took in his intelligent eyes, high forehead, and formal demeanor. Don't make a quick judgment, she warned herself.

They exchanged the usual pleasantries about travel and weather, and then he ordered drinks and after asking her preference, their meal. Four musicians in colorful costumes walked into the room and began playing a Turkish tune. Cass lowered her eyelids and suppressed a sigh of pleasure. American music didn't appeal to her, but there was something about the sound of Anatolian melodies that touched her soul.

Red lentil balls, carrots with yogurt, potato croquettes, pickled stuffed peppers, hummus, and a large basket of bread were set on the table, making Cass smile inwardly.

As they ate, Timur asked questions about America. He told a joke. Cass laughed. He chuckled. A couple passed and the man stopped to greet him. He stood, touched cheek to cheek in the Turkish way, shook hands and introduced Cass.

A waiter poured sauce over thin slices of lamb. As usual when Cass was in this restaurant, she felt as if she'd slipped into a palace. Timur's eyes shone. More raki and wine arrived. Another basket of golden bread appeared as if by the hands of a genie. The drummer's beat was soft, penetrating, enchanting. Cass had forgotten how much she liked Turkish food.

When the baklava and tea were served, Timur finished his third glass of raki, leaned toward Cass and smiled broadly. "So that you know who you're speaking with, I'd like to tell you a story about my father. I've been told he and I are much alike."

Curious, Cass nodded.

"When my father was a soldier after the War of Independence for our great Gazi Ataturk, he had a special duty, to rid the mountaintop near the Black Sea of bandits. My father was the commander. The bandits had been raiding the villages of needed food, often killing innocent villagers in the scavenging of the houses, the crops, and barns.

"They were a well-trained brigade sent in to stop the horrors of these scoundrels. On this night, there was to be a wedding in the village of Dereli. The wedding was that of an important village man's daughter. The ceremony had gone on for the customary week. The family was anxious to share their joy over the excellent match of their daughter with a man from a nearby village who not only owned property, but showed the promise of entering politics one day.

Timur paused for a second, then continued. "My father's brigade knew of this wedding and made precautions to roam the foothills for bandits who might be tempted by the feast to attack. Hours and hours they walked across boulders and perilous paths in the dark under the moonlight watching for any sign of a secret raid. "

He motioned to the waiter for more raki. Cass stopped the waiter from refilling her wine glass.

"Far below they could hear the music, the laughter of the wedding party, and my father as well as his men, wished to join the joyous occasion. But they had a job to do. They would not be done until they had a unique offering for the bride and groom."

He sipped then set down his drink.

"Soon, near a setting surrounded by high cliffs, my father heard a rock tumble down the cliff. He motioned for the troops to stop, and, on his signal they spread out, each finding a hiding place around the ravine to wait."

The man at the next table and the waiter standing behind Timur's chair appeared to be listening intently.

The banker continued. "My father's intuition was right. In less than an hour of patience and silence they heard the snapping of a branch, the scraping of boots. The laughter and music had brought the bandits forward.

"Six men carried rifles; each had a scarf wrapped around his head; each had extra ammunition and grenades strapped to their chests. There was no doubt they were the bandits.

"My father's brigade moved without a sound. The villains, unaware of the brigade's presence, were quickly overcome by the ambush.

"Shortly after, their gifts for the bride and groom were acquired, defused, packaged and tied. With burlap bags hung over their shoulders, the brigade advanced on the fire, the music, the dancing and the fine wedding food.

"As they entered the joyful circle the people hushed, startled at the sight of their uniformed presence. First bowing to the bride in her beautiful red dress and veil and then to the groom in his finery, my father gave the signal to the first line of soldiers carrying the burlap bags, and in unison..." Timur took another drink, then continued. "The men lined up the bags and rolled the bandit's heads into the circle."

"Shit!" Cass couldn't keep her eyes from rounding in disbelief.

The banker, to her surprise, threw his head back and laughed. "You should see your face, my dear. It's priceless."

The man at the next table and the waiter also roared.

Timur wiped his eyes with his napkin. "I believe in America they say, Gotcha. Oh, my dear, how funny."

Cass blushed all the way down to her toenails. This was not the first time she'd been taken in by a jokester. In fact, when she was younger, she was duped all the time. Her eyes narrowed.

Timur's renewed laughter brought more tears to his eyes. "Forgive me, my dear. I just couldn't help myself. You American women are so easily fooled. My father, I assure you, was never a commander, and he most definitely did not cut the heads off a bunch of bandits. He was a, I believe you say, "bean counter" when he served in the military." He chuckled.

Pissed, Cass struggled to keep her expression neutral.

Appearing pleased with himself, Timur began to talk business. "So, the position we have to offer," he said, tapping his lips with his white napkin, "is this: You would be in charge of supervising the building of a housing development project in the Black Sea area."

As her anger subsided, Cass continued to eat.

He picked up his fork and asked the question that she had known would come up: "Do you speak Turkish?"

Cass smiled a pencil smile and shook her head. "No, sorry, only a few words."

He gave no sign he was surprised. "We would, of course, provide you with a translator. I believe your resume` said you were the foreman of one of the wings of a hospital?"

"That's right." Cass leaned forward. "Do you really think Turkish men would trust a woman in such a role?" That was really hard to believe.

"But, of course. We had a woman prime minister. We secularists are progressive."

His eyes were bright. "You are more than qualified for the position. You fit the profile of what we are looking for: someone used to giving orders, someone with experience in many aspects of the building business, and someone who is adventurous enough to want to leave their own country to work abroad. If you want the job, it's yours." He tilted his head to the right.

"And the salary?"

"Ah, yes, the salary. We would match the salary that you would receive doing a similar job in the states. We would also provide housing."

The front door opened. Two Turkish men pulled off their stocking caps, stomped snow off their boots, and dusted their shoulders. One stood as if posed for a photo, a long leg thrown forward, his hands in the pocket of his short leather coat. Chicago gangsters with a capitol G. The taller man locked his eyes with Timur's. Not good. Not good at all. Fully alert, she took another bite of dessert.

"Well?" Timur asked.

"When do you want my answer?"

He sat back in his chair and put his napkin on his plate. His surprise was evident. She suppressed a grin.

"There's an important meeting coming up with the investors. I'd want to know by then. We have other qualified applicants. You have my business card? By all means, call me when you make up your mind or have further questions."

Minutes later, Cass left the restaurant riddled with doubt and suspicion. Why would a foreign company want a non-Turkish–speaking American to do such a job? Man or woman?

She glanced sideways at a man walking too close. His shadowed face was round and pockmarked. She pulled up her jacket collar and hailed a taxi. Maybe she'd been watching too many cop shows, but she was getting the distinct feeling that someone was watching her. And this was definitely a feeling she didn't like.

A string of twinkling lights lit up a plant in a pot reminding her of Christmas. For most, Christmas was a time for memories that made you smile or recall sadness when you didn't get the gift you had asked Santa for. When Cass thought of this holiday, she wanted to spit.

It had been Christmas on the day her mother suggested ten-year-old Cass open the present her father had sent from France where he was attending a conference. He'd included a note instructing Cass to open it in the privacy of her bedroom, but her mother had scoffed at the idea. When Cass refused to open the box, her mother's face reddened. Cass stomped to her bedroom in disgust, slamming the door.

"Just tell him to leave me alone. Please," Cass had begged through the closed door. "That's all I want for Christmas."

"Just open it, for Christ's sake. He's your father," her mother yelled.

So Cass had torn away the curly ribbon and silver paper, then sat for several minutes gnawing at her lower lip. Her mother pushed open the door. Cass lifted the lid of the box. Blood drained from her face. Her heart pounded so hard against her little girl chest that she was sure it would burst out of her like an alien monster that inhabited bodies. The evergreen smell of the wreath behind her head threatened to strangle her. Her fingers trembled.

"Whatever is the matter with you?" her mother said. "Show it to me!"

Teary-eyed, Cass held up the flimsy red negligee.

Her mother gasped.

7

Justina

"Hey, Justina, come with us this time. It's great! You'll love it. Come on. The *hamam* is heavenly!" The colleague rubbed lemon water into her hands, flipping her hair off her shoulder.

Shaking her head, Justina kept her eyes on a bouquet of white carnations on her desk. The woman, she believed, knew that she would never do such a thing, but she loved baiting her.

"Ah, come on...I know you want to go."

Justina said nothing.

A second woman strolled over. "She wants nothing to do with us. She just wants to be by herself. Leave her alone." She pulled on a glove, nodding at the door.

Under her eyelashes, Justina watched the women walk out the door, whispering.

She wished she could say yes, but she couldn't. Something held her back. Some fear. Some dread. Some locked door. Some voice saying that she'd hate it, or it was a sin, and she would be denounced. So she caved into that voice and gave her usual negative response to the women, who shrugged and went off, arm-in-arm, to shop before going to the *hamam* for a luxury treatment.

Justina straightened everything on her desk, pulled on her coat, walked out of the bank and headed toward her apartment. Her head low, her hopes hung on the thought that her husband would be working late tonight, and that she might at least be able to take a leisurely bath in peace.

An open book in the window of a bookshop caught Justina's attention. The delicate, melancholy face of a woman captured on a yellowed page made her breath catch and her eyes widen. It looked like Cass, the only one in Ankara who knew her secret. The snow in front of the window seemed piled into extraordinary, terrifying shapes. She lowered her head and backed away.

Seconds later she readjusted her neck scarf and continued toward her home, thinking about Cass. They had been quite a pair—inseparable. Drunk most of the time. Justina's quick wit making her the life of the party. The life of the party? Her? Her, topless? Justina grimaced with the memory. She stopped and stared at a wide gap in the sidewalk, her gloved hands pressed deeply into her pockets. Eight years. Eight dark years. She had walked out of that gate in Istanbul a changed person.

Going into her apartment building, she took the mail out of their box, rearranged the envelopes so that the pile formed a neat pattern and went up the stairs. On the landing, she straightened the frame of the landscape scene and continued on.

She came to the apartment night after night when her job was done. Sometimes she and Volkan talked about their day, or the snow; sometimes they merely sat, quiet, preoccupied; listening for something in the back of their minds: some voice out of their past, a sound of the sea moving under the earth. Sometimes they played cards. Sometimes they did nothing at all.

Not speaking. Both preoccupied with their own lives.

Volkan sat in the armchair and stared at the TV for hours at a time, as if the whole secret of the universe lay within that screen. Once, as Volkan was passing her with popcorn in his hand, she looked up from her reading and said, "Don't you think it's time to have a child?"

He pointed at her with the bowl. "Do you really think you're ready?"

"When will I ever be?" she asked, pushing back into the protection of her chair, her book, and her silence. A child would make all the difference. That was the truth she clung to.

But that was then.

She slipped into their apartment.

"Justina, is that you?" Volkan was in the living room. The TV was on.

Justina grimaced as she took off her coat, toeing off her shoes. "Yes, yes, it's me." Her words came out soft and billowy as a cloud.

Volkan came into the entry, sipping his drink. He frowned. "I thought you threw that brown suit out ages ago. It doesn't show off your figure, you know. You really should get rid of it."

"My mother bought me this, Volkan, you know that."

"Still, you needn't wear it… she was a psycho. She had appalling taste. God, and look at your hair. It's wild. Absolutely unkempt."

Justina dug her fingernails into her palms, but all she felt was a raindrop's pinprick.

"We're out of limes again," he said. "It seems the least you could do is remember to keep limes in the house."

Her step faltered.

"Hey, don't ignore me. Come here and rub my back. Come on. Don't be grumpy."

Justina closed her eyes and turned. Drifting across the room, she placed herself behind his chair. He bent forward at the waist. Staring into space, she scratched between his shoulder blades.

"There. No, a little lower. To the right. Lower. Ugh, yeah, that's it."

She pressed harder.

"Ah, yes…." With a satisfied moan, he nestled against the chair. "I don't know what I'd do without you, Justina, I really don't."

She patted his shoulder and headed for the kitchen.

"Won't you have a drink with me?"

It was a test. Could she break down and have one drink? What difference would it make? How many years ago had it been since she had been thrown into that black hole? She shuddered. She knew if she drank, her tongue would loosen, and she didn't want Volcan to ever know her secret. The sound of the newscaster's voice boomed and rattled. She shook her head. "No." Why was it so hard for her to say that word?

Volcan sighed and gazed at a news clip. Her eyes shifted to the screen. A man slugged a younger man. Once. Twice. Three times, the scene replayed. And again.

Justina went into the kitchen and leaned against the wall. What difference did anything make? She made her mind go blank, and then lined the vegetables on the counter into a neat pattern. She would prepare perfect rice and sauté vegetables. Thank God, she had finally convinced Volkan to remain out of the kitchen while she prepared the meals. He was such a nuisance. She didn't need a man around meddling and creating a mess. When they were first married, he wanted to help. She had cured him of that. Men did not belong in her kitchen, thank you very much. Nor doing laundry, and certainly not folding clothes. Her mother had trained her to be an excellent wife.

She sliced the knife through the cauliflower. Justina was tired, but not so tired as to ask for help. If she asked once, there would be no end to it. The man would be constantly hanging over her shoulder. She did not want that. She would make dinner. Serve it. Do the dishes while Volkan watched his favorite show, then take a bath and relax.

In her opinion, watching TV was a sin of pleasure, a sign of a weak mind. Like her mother, she preferred to read a chapter of the Bible each night. She had taken up this habit in her cell. Reading and memorizing the verses had helped her to stay sane.

The wild days of her youth were behind her. She would be an epitome of goodness now. She'd found God. She was a born-again Christian who avoided all sinful actions. Cass's face flashed in her mind. She picked up a cherry tomato.

She hadn't thought about Cass for some time. But she had kept all of her cheap black and white tattered journals chronicling their time together. Her pencil scratches she'd never reread. The journals filled a cardboard box, one that had been posted to her aunt's address one day before she was arrested. She supposed they were still gathering dust in her attic, along with other boxes of cherished souvenirs.

Cass had been so naïve then, so weak and vulnerable. Even with the trauma that divorce caused and the dreadful nightmares, she remained positive. Justina admired that quality. It was an attitude Justina had to work at maintaining while it seemed to come natural to Cass. The woman was without guile. She was one of those damn good people you heard about, but seldom met.

Her weakness, being too flexible, was also a strength. Justina often wondered how anyone could use any old toothpaste and any discolored hand cloth to bathe. If Justina's brand of toothpaste ran out, she'd use nothing until she got to a store to buy another tube, and she became flustered if it took too long to find the brand. And she packed her own towel and would use no other. Cass couldn't care what brand of toothpaste she used or who had formerly used a towel, and she rarely became flustered.

It was odd, really. Cass moaned in her sleep and awakened with nightmares, but somehow she was always able to look at the bright side.

Anyway, that's what she projected.

Once they'd been in a bus accident. The bus was hit by another bus and toppled over on its side only a foot from a steep cliff. The driver was killed. Everyone was screaming. Justina began to cry. It was Cass who settled everyone down and got them to help each other climb safely out. In an emergency, she seemed to go calmer. To find a hidden power inside her. That's what impressed Justina most about Cass—that quality she loved the most.

Justina brought the carving knife down on the chopping board. It stuck. She glared menacingly at the vegetables as she dropped them into the skillet of sizzling olive oil. She prided herself on being a fine cook and perfectionist. When she did something, she did it right and wanted no interference. Certainly a Christian virtue, as were timidity, honesty, and humility. Going to a *hamam*, where you were naked in front of other women, where a woman rubbed and kneaded your breasts and bare skin, had to be a sin. It was. Period.

A familiar click made her cock her head. Volkan was setting the table. Good. The fruit bowl. Oh, no! She hurried to the door. "You moved the orange." Not daring to look at Volkan, she rushed to the table and put it back in place.

The orange reminded Justina of her mother, a woman who exhibited bizarre, jealous behavior. In the presence of those who admired her, those she could control, she played

31

the role of best-hostess-of-the-year. Her mother had been an actress before she married. She drew from her vast dramatic material, and assumed a regal angle with her head, while her admirers looked on. But, get a woman near her mother who thought herself her equal, and Rose Sinclair lost all sense of decorum.

Justina would never forget the night when Sheryl, a neighbor who had been under Rose's control for quite some time, had invited her to a dinner party. Her mother saw Sheryl as inferior in intellect, cooking, and rhetorical ability. Since Sheryl accepted her inferiority, she had never been a threat to Rose's standing, but yet another object to sneer at. Sheryl had invited Rose's two young male protégés, one of whom Sheryl was interested in snagging as a lover. The two young men were eight years younger than Sheryl and more than twenty-five years younger than her mother. The fourth guest was a visitor from New York who had just moved into the building. She was Rose's age, but more attractive, soft-looking, a divorced woman with two children. She had money to travel, a sharp wit, and a pleasant attitude. Her positivity, at times, made her seem Pollyannaish, but she was not. She was the type of person who grasped a situation rather quickly, then subtly attempted to rebalance the scale of justice if it were needed, and in this case, it was.

It definitely was.

Rose walked into the living room the night of Sheryl's dinner party and found her two young men in animated conversation with the stranger from New York. Laughter. Warm conversation. Pleasure without her presence. Rose's back bristled. She looked at the guest and saw that the woman had blonde hair (obviously, she was silly and dumb). She also noticed that the stranger's clothes were more expensive than hers (thus she was a materialist) and that she had on makeup (she was shallow).

Justina had been fifteen. She was asked to help serve appetizers and dinner. Seeing her mother's open disdain,

Justina immediately disappeared into the kitchen, where she knew she could watch the drama over the counter that separated the rooms. Sheryl was taking food out of the refrigerator.

The guest shook Rose's hand warmly. Rose smiled, and then sat facing the two men. A place was saved for the hostess beside the man on the sofa.

The woman from New York turned back to the man. "As I was saying, I was amazed at the quality of the apartment in that building. I was invited for a dinner party there last week and, imagine, the doors are oak and have brass handles, quite amazing. It seems they demolished the whole…"

Rose interrupted her. "It's hardly of importance, is it?"

"I'm sorry?" The stranger raised her eyebrows.

"Of what importance is the composition of doors or handles?" Rose tilted her head and looked at the woman over the rim of her glasses.

The woman looked puzzled.

"Oh, of no importance, I'm sure," the woman said, "just a point of interest. I suppose an example of what better apartments consist of, of what one could aspire to."

"Who, my dear, would care about such aspirations?"

"Wouldn't mind having oak doors and brass handles," one young man said.

"Wouldn't be so bad," the other said.

Her mother bristled again and sniffed. Justina giggled. Sheryl picked up a tray and headed for the living room.

"So sorry, these are a bit overcooked." She passed around what looked like perfect mushroom appetizers.

"That's all right, my dear," Rose said, "you'll learn to use the oven one of these days."

The New Yorker smiled at Sheryl. "These look perfect to me."

Rose glared at her. Sheryl nodded her gratitude.

33

The stranger addressed the men, "For me, it's heaven to be here."

"If this is heaven for you, my dear, you must have led a very narrow life." Rose's expression was wooden.

"I don't believe there is a heaven, but if I did, Turkey would be one of my models." She turned to the men, "When I was in India..." She talked on and on, telling stories while the men and Sheryl (now seated) listened with full attention. Justina leaned against the counter to catch every word.

Not Rose. She slumped back in her chair and sneered. Her body and facial expressions clearly indicated that she thought the stranger had no ability to tell an intelligent, engaging story. She fell far below Rose's critical expectations of what great storytelling should be. She herself, Rose, would be an accomplished storyteller. But, of course, she wasn't. She would never be, because such a frivolous thing was beneath her.

Justina's cheeks reddened.

The New Yorker tapped an orange in the fruit bowl sitting on the end table beside her chair as she talked.

"Humph!" Rose finally said, causing the stranger to stop her latest story in mid-sentence.

"Yes?" the woman asked, grasping the orange.

"Do you really think that? I mean, it seems so, so childish!"

The women gazed at each other, neither blinking.

"Yes, well, I suppose, to some it might be, but to me and to many others in the world..." The stranger continued while Rose seethed.

When the dessert Rose brought was served, Rose, even though she knew it was perfect, said it was possibly a tad bit dry.

"That's okay, I like my cake dry," one man said.

"Carrot cake?" the woman said. "Does that mean you have a vegetable grater? I'm incredibly impressed. Oh, and I like cake dry, as well. Not to worry."

Justina couldn't help but laugh.

With narrowed eyes, her mother marched into the kitchen, grabbed Justina's arm, and marched her out of the room.

"But, Mother, I promised I would help clean up," Justina protested.

Fuming, Rose pushed her through the front door.

Justina had watched the scene as if she were viewing a play. Seeing her mother in the role of a jealous, bitter woman helped her to break away from her control. It had been an important evening for her as a teenager. No longer was she a "Sheryl" around her mother. She worked hard from that night forward to stand up to her mother's power. An orange took on a different meaning.

For months Justina ate one orange a day, relishing each juicy bite. Then years later she made the mistake of her life. She stole and was caught.

In prison Justina learned how to deal with pain. It was simple: Place your hands on your knees or on the arms of a chair, turn the palms upward, separate the fingers and breathe deeply. The method worked so well that, once she was released, she used no Novocain or gas at the dental office, even for a root canal. But sometimes, and lately it was happening more often, the method didn't work, or she was caught off-guard by the velocity of the inner attack. Her control would dissolve like an aspirin in a glass of water. Sometimes, she lost track of time and of her actions and feared for her sanity.

Days went by and she would be fine, so she would grow less concerned. Her mother once said, as if her daughter hadn't lived with her all those years: "I can handle anything. Just bring it on. I won't let those bastards get me down." And her mother hadn't. When her incurable cancer was diagnosed, she refused to let the monster win. Instead, she drove her car over the railroad tracks and stopped, leaving a note of farewell and triumph over the beast that dared attempt to control her. The way things were now, Justina fought for that same sense of control, not wanting to give in to that inner pain.

She bent her head, drawing a circle with one finger on the countertop, moving the finger around and around the circle, saying the words aloud, as though they were important, louder this time, to penetrate what she knew no one could hear. "I won't let that bastard get me down." She glanced at the doorway and her heart caught. Looking shocked, Volkan was watching.

Justina lowered her gaze and rounded her shoulders. Without a word, Volkan turned and walked away.

She recalled her mother carefully reading the train schedule the morning of her suicide, her coffee cup steaming on the table in front of her. Justina had stood behind her mother, kneading her shoulders, wanting to take the poison of cancer into herself. Justina remembered her saying: "You must think of others, Justina, when you make a decision. Remember that."

They sawed through the car to get her out and laid her on a stretcher, only feet in front of Justina's shaking body. When the paramedics lifted her, their muscles bulged with her weight.

Her mother would never have chosen a slow death, one that would have eaten away her dignity and self-respect. Justina had no reason to think her mother was weak. It was a choice. Her way. The other way would have made no sense.

Once more Justina heard her mother's words spoken softly, but firmly: Don't let the bastards get you down.

Shaking her head, Justina tossed aside the thoughts of her mother. After all, she had been dead for over ten years now. Justina would never be like her, thank God. Her mother was pretentious, a trait Justina could never tolerate. Justina often wondered if the stranger from New York would have given Rose another chance to be civil. She doubted it. Why should she?

A loud sigh came from her husband. He would want sex tonight. She slipped the dishtowel "just so" over the rack. She would have to remember to put a clean towel on the nightstand. She hated stained sheets; even more, she hated the dreadful feeling of guilt. He gave her a life. Why couldn't she appreciate it? But having sex with him made her feel like a prostitute. Her cell phone rang.

Paling, she turned.

A stabbing pain penetrated; quickly she held out the palms of her hands. As if the pain were a cigarette, she breathed in deeply and stood perfectly still. She coughed and picked up the phone.

"Hello."

"Did you answer a roommate wanted ad?"

Justina shot a glance to her husband. He was out of earshot. With lowered voice, she asked if she could return the call.

8

Cass

Waiting to leave for the meeting with Justina, Cass was so nervous she had been unable to eat breakfast.

She reached into her bag and pulled out a dog-eared photo of Justina and herself taken in southern Turkey. They were wearing black and white helmets and biking gear—a style that showed off their youthful, shapely bodies. They were smiling. Looking cool. Strong. Like seasoned travelers. Justina had her arm around Cass. Cass's hands were folded in front of her. Both had their chestnut hair hanging over their shoulders. They looked fresh, intelligent, untroubled; ready for anything that life dished out.

Cass had been nineteen. Justina twe
exhilarating time—a time of experimen{
experiences, especially for Cass who had lec

Their mothers, Justina had assured Cas
opportunities they had. Here they were t
Turkey and Greece with the only responsibilities being to
make sure they had a place to sleep at night, food, and
enough money for their habits. Which really meant Justina's
habit as she was a steady pot smoker. Cass had tried
smoking pot only once.   It had made her lungs hurt, so she
had quit. She had only taken up cigarette smoking two years
ago. She had a feeling that smoking pot wouldn't be the
same experience it had been then, but to date, she'd had no
urge to try it.

"Celebrate, woman. Celebrate every day you're alive,"
Justina had told Cass so often it became a mantra.

How many times over the last years had Cass asked
herself, "What would Justina do in this situation?" More
than she wanted to count. It had been the therapist who
convinced her that that was a bad habit. "Figure out what it
is you would do, Cass. That's when it will be right." The
problem was, Cass just hadn't known what she should do.
Not then. Not always now.

Cass ran her finger over the photo, then dropped it into
her bag again.

As she hurried to the park she dropped lira into every
beggar's box she passed, hoping to bring good luck her way.
It had taken her years to accept that her superstitious self
was acceptable.

The sky above the treetops was streaked with gold,
lavender, and dusty pink. The open-air park bushes and bare
branches of the trees glistened from being coated with
slivers of ice. But the day was warming, the ice was
beginning to melt. Cass was optimistic as she entered the
park.

39

Justina sat at an outside table. Her now bleached-blonde hair took Cass aback and made her think of Marilyn Monroe. Justina in a skirt? Hmm. Cass pulled out a chair and sat quickly. "I'm so..."

"Yeah, me too..." Justina mumbled.

Justina's solemn attitude made Cass's excitement drop a notch. She lowered her head, hiding her disappointment. A waiter appeared. Cass ordered a soda. Justina was already sipping from a cup.

Cass cleared her throat. "I came here to... Oh, I'm not sure why I came."

"Are any of us ever sure of anything?"

Cass, feeling herself already falling under Justina's stronger personality, blanched and said nothing.

Justina glanced at the yellow carnation in the vase at the center of the table, then at Cass. She twisted the gold band on her third finger of her left hand. The silence was awkward and was broken by a very nervous Cass. Talking rapidly, she told Justina about her new life as a restorer of homes and builder of hospitals, letting the words gush out, hardly knowing what she was saying.

Justina listened and watched her every move, but her lips remained set. Cass expected amazement and admiration for her transformation from a girlie-girl to a woman working in a man's world, but got none. She slumped back in her chair, exhausted from trying to impress her old friend who still sat silently gazing at her with hardly a spark of anything in her eyes, surrounded by an aura of steely reserve.

Frustrated, Cass glanced at Justina's hand and asked a question she knew the answer to. "So, you're married?"

Justina turned her attention to the park pond, then slowly looked at Cass with an intensity that made Cass blink. "Yes." Her eyes were the color of a china plate Cass's mother owned.

"And?" Cass asked.

"And, nothing. That's all." Justina straightened her shoulders. "And you? Did you marry again?"

Cass shook her head. "Nah. I've been too busy. Besides, once was enough."

Last night before falling into a fitful sleep, Cass had allowed herself to see the two of them enjoying this rapidly developing country together again. She imagined that Justina and she would be equal guides, charting the course for different adventures, revisiting places and laughing over old memories.

"You ever think that…"

Justina interrupted her again. "No. Never."

Cass caught her breath and changed the subject. "Kids?"

"Not yet. But we're thinking about starting a family."

"You'll make a great mom. A job?"

"I work in a bank. Working internationally is stimulating. I'm lucky really…" Her words drifted away.

"I…"

"I love my job."

"I was in jail in Mexico. I heard that you got caught after I got back to the states." Cass picked up her glass. "How long did you have to stay in the...that place?"

Justina rubbed her forehead. "The whole nine yards—eight years." She looked at her cup, at the tiny silver-plated spoon, but not at Cass.

Cass reached for one of Justina's hands.

Justina pulled away, looking everywhere but at Cass.

Cass suppressed a sigh. Why had she done that?

"Does your husband know?"

Looking stunned, Justina checked her watch. "Oh, I have to run." She pushed back her chair.

Oh, no. Not yet…Cass half-stood. "But, we'll meet again?"

"Uh…" Justina hesitated. "Well, let me talk to my husband. Let me ask his schedule. Of course, I want you to meet him and see my home. Let me call you, we'll have you over for dinner. It's been great seeing you again, it really has."

Justina's hug was brief, without warmth. She turned and fled.

The blood rushed from Cass's head, leaving her dazed. "Justina?"

Justina stopped, turned. "Yes?"

"I *can* call you again?"

Justina ran her fingers through her dyed hair, nodded and was gone.

No discussion of the past. No forgiveness. No advice about the job offer. No rekindled friendship.

No, nothing.

Crestfallen, Cass focused on the small pond. A white swan raised its wings. One was injured. She wondered if in Turkey there were humane societies to take care of such animals. The bird shook its head and swam in a circle. She paid the bill, took a piece of bread out of the wicker basket on the table, and went to a snow-dusted wooden bench.

Sitting, she tore the bread apart, tossing bits into the dark icy water. The swans swarmed, swallowing the offering almost before it landed. Cass felt like a failure. She'd come to Ankara to apologize to Justina, and she hadn't been able to get the words out. Where was her backbone? Seeing Justina after all these years was just too big of a shock. She should take the job. That would give her the time she needed to make things right. But she would not do that without advice.

Head down, hands in pockets, Cass left the park to stroll the streets. She passed expensive clothing stores, a clean, efficient subway, a modern supermarket. Flakes of snow dampened her hair and shoulders. She walked into a department store and hesitated at a display of stacked linens and thought of Ulus, the old area of the city. Would Umit and his brother still be at their shop?

42

Skirting through the crowd, she took the escalator. At the bottom, most of the people veered right toward the grocery section. She headed toward the entrance, then turned north toward Ulus. She kept an eye on the sidewalks; a deep hole in the cement could appear anywhere.

A man dressed in beggar's clothes and a knitted skull cap sat on the sidewalk, his bandaged knee sticking out. A cardboard box was pressed against his leg. Saddened, she reached into her bag, pulled out two bills and bending at her knees, slipped them into his box. The man's head did not move.

Odd. Was that a camera click? She swore it was the click of a camera. She looked all around, saw no one photographing her, nodded at the beggar, stood straight and walked into a crowd to catch a *dolmush*. The first van was full. She took the second.

Cass settled beside a man with a gray beard and dark suit. He stood immediately and changed seats. She refused to acknowledge the insult. Justina had said that Western women alone were often thought of as whores by fundamentalists. She knew she was no whore. In fact, she wasn't even a tad bit loose. She had an old-fashioned belief that love was much more important than sex. Not that she was a prude; she just wasn't someone who slept around. The ride was less than fifteen minutes. She glanced back at the elderly Turk who refused to meet her gaze, hopped off and continued her walk.

Men stood on the sidewalks selling their wares on tiny portable tables, or had them lined up neatly on small blankets: inexpensive watches, Ataturk key chains, billfolds, socks, combs, batteries, scarves, blue evil eyes, anything one could name was for sale. Flowers and plants were sold on street corners or from the back of red, yellow, and blue painted trucks. Tomatoes, apples, strawberries, and oranges were stacked into pyramids. Dried flowers hung from the top of the stands creating an enticing garden effect.

43

Cass stopped and lit a cigarette. Smoking was a habit that could kill you. She should stop, but there were a lot of things she should do.

A young boy with cropped hair passed, carrying a large tray of golden, salty *simits* on his head. With the grace of a gazelle, the boy slipped through the crowd, stopping only occasionally for a customer. Men walked arm-in-arm. Women did the same. Cass passed a bus stop where people crowded shoulder-to-shoulder, so close that she could smell their sweat. And all the while, she felt preoccupied by her unsatisfying conversation with Justina.

After leaving her husband, she'd had one true friend and that was Justina. She would make amends with Justina. She would. It wasn't Umit she wanted advice from. It was Justina. She would use this reason to call her again.

She dropped her cigarette butt, ground it under her boot, and trekked back to her apartment.

9

Justina

Justina's step was light as she went down the stairs of the apartment building in Gasiomanpasa where she'd been interviewed as a roommate. The questions the two women had asked weren't too personal. That part was easy enough. A simple lie. Not so damning, but so soon? Could she really be ready to leave her husband by then?

Seeing Cass had cinched her decision. It had been difficult to sit across from her and be reminded of who she had once been. Cass seemed so self-assured. Hearing that she was a contractor was like hearing that Minnie Mouse was now Mrs. Hulk. While Cass had had inner strength when she knew her, she certainly had not been practical or physically strong. She'd had trouble hauling her backpack onto her back and had never figured out how to buy a bus ticket or read a map. Justina couldn't imagine her wielding a hammer or knowing anything about construction. Incredible. The woman was a walking ad that change was possible.

The only other contractor she had known was a man she met from Cappadocia before she was married to Volkan. He fucked her so many different ways every time they were together that she jokingly told him she feared he would have a heart attack, or that she would. The fact that he counted the ways might be an irritant to some, but she found it charming and so very male. One night the bed, to their wild laughter and raucous activity, disintegrated beneath them. But that didn't stop him or her, for that matter. He was feverish to marry her and be taken to America. When he insisted that she shave her pubic hair for cleanliness reasons, she balked and told him she could never marry such a strict Islamic man. He accused her of only wanting to fuck him, which after the first night together was more than true. They'd parted the last time after a romantic dance.

Justina let out a large puff of air. Maybe with time she would get back to her former free-spirited self. She could only hope. If Cass could find the strong woman inside her, surely she'd find her again too.

She remembered one of the women who interviewed her as a prospective roommate. Sevgi Arslan. She was the kind of woman who would help Justina the most. She recalled the Turkish woman's confidence as she had entered the bank last week, and was surprised when she realized how young she was. She couldn't be more than eighteen. She envied her. The Turkish woman was just the type she needed to be around right now. Independent and obviously going places.

When the snowflakes thickened and the wind picked up, Justina hailed a cab and gave the address of her apartment across the city. She knew that she would spend a sleepless night. After paying the driver, she left the cab, looking up.

Their apartment lights were out. Volkan must have worked late again. Excellent.

A Mercedes pulled up to the curb. A man stepped out. Justina caught her breath as she stared at a face she hadn't seen in years.

"Why, Justina, is that you?"

Justina nodded but could not speak.

"Why, I can hardly believe my eyes. What a surprise. And just what I need right now, an old friend to talk to. I was going to visit an employee of mine, but this is so much better. Please, please, let me take you for a drink."

Timur put his hand on her elbow and helped her into the back seat of the car. She cleared her throat and forced herself to speak.

"Timur, I…" she stammered. "How long have you been in Ankara?"

"Why I've lived here for only a few weeks now. I'm a bank manager, just transferred from Istanbul. And you?"

"I've lived here for a couple of years. I work for a bank as well."

"Really, how interesting. "Which one?"

"Is Bank." She looked out the window, thinking of her husband, her boss, her job, and the new life she planned.

"Really? Which branch?"

"Ataturk Caddessi," she said, sinking back into the seat, trying to make herself disappear.

"But that's too, too delicious," Timur said, smiling. "One of my best friends is the bank manager, Osman Celik. You know him, of course."

Justina lowered her head. "I'm his administrative secretary."

"Oh my, I can't believe my luck running into you." He leaned forward and touched the back of the front seat.

"Here stop, here," he commanded. The driver pulled to the curb.

47

"Come. Let's go into this bar. Let me fill you in on the project. I may even have a little favor to ask you." He chuckled as he helped her out of the cab.

Putting his hand on her back, he ushered her into the darkened room. Without asking what she wanted, he ordered drinks. Justina said nothing. All she could think about was that there were two people now in Ankara who knew her past. Timur was animated. He talked on and on. Justina did not touch her glass. Somewhere down a long, thin tunnel, she heard the words: Housing. Osman Celik. Timur asked a question that Justina didn't hear.

Justina continued to be unable to speak.

Apparently taking her silence for agreement, Timur smiled a toothy smile. "Great! Great I knew my stars were aligned today." He stood and dropped bills on the table.

"I'll call you soon. It'll be like old times. There's a lot of money in this, Justina," he said, chuckling. "Oh, and, Justina, you won't believe this, but guess who'll be our partner?" With relish, he rubbed his hands together. "Your old friend, Cass Griffith. I had lunch with her. Did you know she's a successful contractor now? I was so surprised when her name popped up on our search for American prospects. I couldn't mistake that face. And those long legs. Unforgettable. Stunning. Amazing, huh? Us working together again."

Justina had planned the robbery. Naïve Cass was kept uninformed of the details and was only to drive the getaway car. Justina had arranged for Timur to fence the stolen items. Like Cass, he was never implicated in the crime.

Justina was dumbfounded. Was this for real? Cass was a criminal?

"She didn't know me of course. How could she? We never actually met. I saw her once with you at a movie. You two looked quite happy. I never forget a face. This will be a win-win situation, don't you agree?"

Justina nodded.

He grinned and withdrew his wallet. "Forgive me, but I must show you a picture of my children. This is…"

But Justina again no longer heard his words.

10

Justina

Later, at her home, Justina gazed steadily into her dresser drawer as if staring at it would make everything in it transport to the new apartment. An unopened bottle of birth control pills lay in the center. Picking up the container, she squeezed it with all of her strength, but the solid bottle seemed to mock her. She tossed it on top a stack of shirts and pushed the drawer shut. She had one suitcase to put all of her clothes and belongings in, only one. She had called the new roommate, Sevgi, to say she had decided to take the apartment. Could she move in immediately? Yes. Excellent.

And, so, she was going. Tomorrow she would stop by her new roommate's workplace and give her a deposit. Justina closed the door gently. She could never tell Volkan her plans. She must first move out. She feared he would overpower her decision with his protests, his manipulative ways. Her shoulders sagged. She felt lethargic, weighted. She had no idea what she was going to do about Timur and his scheme. Her body trembled with the thought.

Tonight while Volkan was at a meeting she would pack.

Her heart, especially now that she had made her decision, was pounding as loudly as an early morning knock on her door. Her temperature might even be a few degrees higher than normal—she'd felt panicky and anxious for so long that the feelings had become far too familiar. Aside from an occasional rapid blinking of her left eye, her every gesture was measured and calm. For all the world knew, she might have been a model of serenity. But Justina was aware of a dark jester tapping on her conscience, grinning fiercely, delighted to startle and alarm her. She'd learned to control this smiling, white-faced, painted buffoon for hours at a time, her need for control guiding her actions. For the most part, she kept the jester's wicked notions caged. On other occasions, the fool practiced his curious ability to sneak up on her and deliver a painful, body-bending shock.

Today she would buy another suitcase. Two would be sufficient. Anything she could not get into two, she would leave behind. Suddenly, she inhaled; a sharp pain stabbed at her chest, but as quickly as it came, it went. "I can do it, I *can* do this," she assured herself in a whisper.

The front door opened and closed again. Volkan, who had gone to the nearby grocery for cigarettes, walked across the living room floor, moving quickly. Arrested in motion, she listened for his footsteps coming toward the bedroom until the sound was drowned out by the clanking and banging of a garbage truck. The workers shouted, busy at their work, taking away the week's refuse.

"Justina, come on. We'll be late."

She pretended not to hear.

"Hurry up!"

Straightening her shoulders, she raised her head. "I'm coming. Be right there!" She turned and with tiny, hesitant steps left the room.

"Why, Justina, you look so different this morning. Radiant. You must have had a good night's sleep," Volkan said, taking her arm.

Justina's smile was too brilliant and the sparkle in her eyes held a hint of madness.

Volkan eyed his wife as they walked down the stairs to the street. "Have you heard of a possible promotion at the bank?"

"No, nothing."

Volkan's right eyebrow arched. "You're still taking your pills, aren't you?"

"Of course," she lied. She had not taken a pill in over three months. "In fact, I've decided I don't want children."

Suspicion darkened Timur's tone of voice. "And why not?"

"Oh, it would be a hindrance to me; I mean, to us, right now, don't you think?"

Volkan visibly relaxed. "Absolutely. I'm so glad you see that now. When we are making more money, that's when the time will be right. By the way, there's a company dinner Saturday night. Do stop and buy yourself a new dress. The big shots are coming from Istanbul. I want to make a good impression."

The blood drained from her head. Saturday? "Oh, I think my black dress will do. It's very smart," she said absently.

"No, no…" He reached into his wallet and began pulling out several bills. "Here's plenty to buy something special for the evening."

"Oh, okay, if it means so much to you. Maybe I'll have a new haircut, as well." Her voice was distant.

The amount he gave her as they settled in the taxi, she realized, would cover the price of the new suitcase and more. The paper felt as thin as a butterfly's wings.

"Maybe if we're lucky, by this time next year we'll be able to afford a car. Wouldn't that be grand? To own a car. We could take weekend trips. Now, don't forget to smile warmly at your boss today and do exactly what he says. Maybe this week will be our lucky turn-around week."

"Yes, maybe it will." Justina stared out the taxi window. "Volkan?" Her voice was as soft as a snowflake.

"Yes, my dear."

She looked at the large figure of her husband sitting beside her, thought of her lie. So many women would be thrilled to have him for a husband. Was she crazy like her mother? "Oh, nothing, nothing," she finally said, fingering her skirt.

She wished that she could be happy with this man. Life would be so much easier. But she could not keep up the deception any longer. Nor did she have the strength to counter his protests. Maybe in the future when she was away from him for a while, she would be stronger and could be honest. Right now she just needed to get away. She told herself this repeatedly as the taxi driver honked madly at a stalled car in the early morning rush hour traffic.

When did she stop thinking of herself as "I"? Justina wondered. When had she become a "we"? Certain religions stated that thinking in terms of *we* is the highest form of humanity. But was that true? If she were not an I, but only a we, could she ever make a decision that was best for her? Wouldn't she always be entrapped in *we*? Wasn't that a form of imprisonment? *We* do this because it was best for *us*? *We* don't do this because it was best for *us*. What about Justina?

Didn't Justina count?

"We have a bright future ahead, Justina."

Justina plucked a loose thread from her skirt. One of the first things she was planning to do was change her wardrobe. She hated all the skirts. She wanted to buy, no *would* buy five pairs of jeans. One for each day of the work week. And her hair. She hated the blonde color. "Yes, I'm sure you're right, Volkan."

"Oh, I *am* right. Turkey is at the cusp of change and development and we are in the throes of things; isn't that exciting?"

"Of course." The clown in her head laughed.

"Hey, where is that Justina I heard earlier? Stiffen that upper lip, as the American's say, woman. Show your stuff. Be the woman I married."

Justina dutifully sat straighter in the seat. "You're correct, of course. The world is large, full of new experiences, new people, change," she said with conviction.

"You bet. That's the spirit!" The taxi came to a stop and Justina opened the door.

"Smile brightly!" Volkan called before the taxi sped away.

Justina found herself needing to hold on to chairs and desks as she made her way to her computer. Her coworkers noticed something was wrong or at least different, but not her boss. He had not yet come in this morning. He was not behind his desk when Justina went into his office to deliver some documents. She set the papers near his pearl-handled letter opener.

It reminded her of her mother and the knife incident. Her mother had been a closet kleptomaniac. Totally uncontrollable and unreasonable, her actions were a constant embarrassment to Justina and to her father.

Justina would never forget the time a neighbor, Mrs. White, had come to her house and asked to look in their kitchen. She had a favorite paring knife made in England that she had purchased while abroad. It had come up missing right after her mother had left her home. Mrs. White remembered leaving Justina's mother in the kitchen while she answered the telephone. She said she had been slicing tomatoes from her garden for dinner while Justina's mother read to her an article from the newspaper. The doorbell rang and she left the room to answer it. When she got back, the knife was gone; she thought nothing of it until later.

Mrs. White was apologetic and embarrassed to be confronting the teenage daughter, but there had been other times that she had suspected that Justina's mother was stealing from her house. The missing knife was the last straw.

Justina had, of course, stood back and allowed the woman to enter the kitchen. Her mother was out. The neighbor opened the top drawer near the sink and there was the knife she had described, standing in the row of other neatly placed knives, totally mismatched from the rest. Justina and the woman stared down into the drawer for several moments before Justina reached in and took out the offending knife. Mrs. White shook her head in sympathy and left the house without a word.

Justina had gone to her bedroom and cried her shame into her pillow. It had not been the first time such a thing had happened. It would not be the last. The day her mother killed herself was the day the stealing ended.

Justina would not be like her mother, she told herself. Never.

Justina's right hand was lost in the folds of the skirt of her dress as she walked out of the office, pulling the door closed.

"Would you get me a cup of tea, Justina?"

Justina ignored him and went to her desk.

The coworker to her right swiveled in her chair. "Justina, are you finally pregnant?"

"No!"

"Are you sure? Your skin is shining."

"No, I've just made a big decision this morning, that's all."

"Big? Do tell!"

"I'm sorry, I have work to do." Justina shook her head in mock disgust, adjusting her reading glasses.

Later, Justina had a waking dream. She was holding the letter opener. Blood dripped from the tip. Cass, Timur, and Volkan lay bleeding on the floor.

11

Cass

Cass pocketed her cell phone. The banker had called. He wanted her to meet the other investors. He would pick her up Monday night. Great. Just great. And still no info.

Since repeatedly phoning Justina led to no success, Cass decided it was time to visit Umit Yilmaz, the carpet dealer who she constantly had to remind herself was not her father. He was the only Turkish person that she knew beyond a handshake in Ankara.

Within blocks of leaving the apartment, she felt as if she were being followed. She crisscrossed the crowded sidewalk, hoping to discourage the man or men.

Cass knew that one problem in Turkey was that there were too many unemployed, bored young men roaming the streets. Men, who in the states would most likely be in college or working. In Turkey there were far more applicants for college than there were colleges and few jobs. Since it was broad daylight, she assumed this was why she was being followed. She was relatively young. Attractive. Alone. Obviously an American. She didn't feel frightened, merely annoyed by the need to watch her back.

"Whew!" She swiped her brow, took the last steep step in the flight of stairs leading to the ancient castle and headed for a bench. Drawing out her travel journal, she wrote: To take the job or not, that is the question. She grimaced, closed the notebook and slid it into her pocket. Writing had always been a way to see how deep her convictions were. When she was young and dumb, she used it to decide how much she cared for a guy or what color dress to buy by how much she wrote about it in her journal.

Nearby, a worker in an inexpensive business suit cleared the sidewalk with a short-handled shovel. A girl in a flowered headscarf leaned on the shoulder of a soldier. Olive-skinned children played with a red ball embossed with a crescent moon and a star. A man in a turban sat on a low-footed pine stool behind an intricately inlaid, brass shoeshine kit. Snowflakes created a swaying lace curtain. Cass closed her eyes, counted breaths, and felt lifted and fused in a soul bath.

She opened her journal again and began to free write. This time it was about Turkey, not the job. When her flashbacks had become more frequent, more frightening, it had been journal writing that had saved her from going mad and that had led her to therapy. She wrote fast, letting her imagination overtake her reason. After several minutes, she closed the journal and returned it to her purse, then stood. The path wound through the park. Taking a right, she faced a museum behind a tall, wrought-iron fence. A group of Asian tourists stepped down from a shining tour bus, some looking at brochures; others talking among themselves, while a man and woman locked arm-in-arm strolled toward the entrance. Cass, thoroughly enjoying the walk she'd taken several times before on her previous visit, faced uphill and continued to climb.

Kilims and intricately woven bags hung from doorframes. Copper pots and pitchers were stacked on the sidewalks of the cobblestone street. A rack of blue evil eyes of various sizes and shapes stood to one side of a shop, making Justina's face appeared in her mind.   She hurried on. A taxi driver banged on the horn. Cass snapped her head in the upward Turkish gesture for "no" and moved on.

She stopped in front of three barrels of nuts.

"*Buyrun*," the Turkish man said, welcoming her.

"*Merhaba* (Hello)." She smiled and pointed. The olive-skinned man grinned and held up a bag. She nodded.

"*Americalium*?"

"*Evet. Ya siz*?"

"*Sayah Denis*," His eyes sparkled with pride.

"Ah, near the Black Sea?"

He bowed.

Vowing to learn more Turkish if she decided to remain, she held up the bag in way of farewell.

Three women in headscarves walked toward her arm-in-arm talking in low tones. They wore street-length, pale green coats and intricately patterned headscarves. Their eyes remained on the ground as they neared and passed. Cass heard a giggle and the word "*Americalium*" whispered. She shelled a nut and tossed it in her mouth, grinning. Even if she tried, she knew she could not conceal the fact she was an American. It was stamped into the way she walked, the way she held her shoulders, her dress, her hairstyle, her very being.

At the top of the next hill she headed south toward the three-hundred-year-old mosque and shop. Ten years was a long time. Would the shop still be there? The brothers?

Stuffing the brown paper bag of nuts into her pocket, she stepped inside to the sound of a small bell. A mixture of

59

thrill and fear tapped at her heart. A dark, mahogany canopy bed blocked the front window from view. Delicate white-cotton lace curtains hung from the top of the wooden frame. Wool and silk carpets, flat weaves, and *kilim* pillows were thrown haphazardly on the bed. Antique copper war helmets. Intricately carved furniture. Ceiling-high stacks of carpets and other *kilims* completed the picture. As she took in the sight, Cass gripped and released her fingers, remembering.

It was here where she had met Justina. Cass had been traveling around aimlessly for a couple of weeks and was staying at a nearby youth hostel. Feeling the need for a cup of tea and conversation, she strolled into the open door. Justina was sitting on a stack of carpets, sipping tea and talking with an older man. The shop was lit only by a single lamp and the effect was magical for Cass who had once loved reading the *Tales of the Arabian Nights*. Justina and the man glanced her way, but it was another man who greeted Cass and offered her tea. She accepted and went to the pile of carpets and sat. Justina acknowledged her with a nod but continued her conversation.

After a few moments their eyes met. From that night on, Justina became Cass's exclamation point as they traveled about the country. It was Umit who gave Justina and Cass the evil eyes that night. Cass, the ditz (the role she had not yet shed) had promptly lost hers, but Justina carried hers in her pocket everywhere they went.

Today two young boys sat on rush-seated chairs beyond the iron, pot-bellied stove holding needles. Multi-colored strips of yarn covered their knees. The boys held the needles in midair as they gazed at her with expressions of curiosity. They wore black wool dress pants and short-sleeved plaid shirts. Their hair was cropped close. Cass smiled at them good-naturedly and nodded. She tossed a glance into the adjoining room, but saw no one else.

"*Merhaba*. Umit?"

The boys, obviously anxious to please, spoke in unison. "*Sonra*."

One stood and walked to her, tapping his watch dial. His pants were two inches too short. "*Sonra*," he repeated, pointing to the hands of his watch.

"*Evet, evet*," Cass said, "*Tamam, sonra.*" She walked out the door. She had understood; he would be back later—*sonra*—in about a half-hour.

Cass turned right and went up the hill passing several other carpet and antique shops. Occasionally, she raised her hand to ward off beaming, enthusiastic hawkers who wanted to sell her their wares. Glancing over her shoulder, she saw no suspicious male. But she felt on edge. She went left and hurried down the hill toward the museum, paying the entry fee.

The stone archway framed a blue sky with cumulus white clouds. She took another step, frowned, and rubbed her neck. Her gaze shot around the courtyard. Something was wrong. What was it?

A man in a red shirt, blue jeans, and a black leather jacket quickly looked away.

Cass hurried into the room made of thick stone walls. Disturbed by the telltale itch at the base of her hairline, she scratched at her neck again.

The banker having her followed? But why would he want to know her every move? No, she reasoned, it's just some foolish man who has nothing else to do with his time.

Inside, she strolled toward a pair of Hittite ritual vessels in the form of bulls. She shot a look over her shoulder. No one. Nothing. Still…

The bulls' magnificent horns pointed outward and upward toward the sky, as if reaching for a blessing from the gods. The clay had been molded to fashion graceful neck muscles attached to strong bodies. An opening for wine was molded into their necks. The figures weren't more than thirty-six inches high, but they were noble beasts. She

61

leaned in to read the inscription: 14th Century BC. Still bent forward and suspicious, she scanned the room.

Looking from right to left, she hesitated in front of a Hittite tombstone of a man and woman standing arm-in-arm, serene, content. Their hands grasped a bunch of grapes and other unknown fruit. A flash of red caught her eye. Her hand shot to her neck. Her gaze snapped around the room. Her suspicions grew. She stepped into a group of German tourists straining to hear the words of their guide.

The crowd gushed forward. Cass hugged the center. Near the entrance, she dashed for the door then stopped. With narrowed eyes she retraced her steps and placing her hands on her hips, faced the man in the red shirt.

"Don't follow me. Understand? If you do, I'll call the *Polis*, the cops!"

She swiveled around and marched away, smiling.

12

Cass

The *muezzin's* doleful call to prayer reverberated as Cass entered the carpet shop built under the three-hundred-year-old mosque. The tinging of the bell attached to the front door made her scalp feel as if it were invaded by a centipede. A warning?

Cass told herself to stop being foolish. An over-weight, long-haired cat slept on a sofa. Slippers scratched against wood. Glancing toward an interior door, she put her hand back on the doorknob. Perhaps she shouldn't have come. Maybe, just maybe, she wasn't ready to face Umit.

Umit stepped out of the room and beamed. "Ah, Cass Griffith, so you have returned to Turkey?" He welcomed her so warmly that Cass allowed him to pull her into the room.

"I wasn't sure you'd remember me," she said.

He laughed. "How could I forget you? You are like a daughter to me. Come sit, let's have tea. Apple? Normal?" He motioned to the boys in the corner.

"Normal."

The boys scurried out the door as Umit and Cass went to sit on a carpet-draped bench. She could see Ali in a back room rearranging boxes.

"How long has it been?" Umit asked.

"Over ten years. I was a kid then. I'm twenty-nine now."

They chatted while they sweetened the tea and with care adjusted the tulip-shaped glasses on the saucers.

When the front doorbell jingled, Umit excused himself and hurried away. Cass leaned back against a pillow. Her eyes fell on an exquisite *kilim* hanging on the far wall. Thinking of Justina who loved these thin woven rugs, she stood, went to the rug and traced the star-shaped design of the symbols. The flat weave was no more than two feet wide and about five feet long. Threads of orange wool outlined stars. Geometric shapes looked like humans holding hands.

Umit reentered. "Come, I want you to see something." He lifted a rug hanging in the middle of a wall, uncovering a wooden door.

Intrigued, Cass set down her tea glass, and ducking, slipped inside.

The room was lit by table lamps. The rugs, copper pots and pans, furniture, statues, and jewelry must be hundreds of years old. Cass had never seen so much beauty in one place, not even in a museum and she said so.

"These pieces were passed down from my family or purchased in the eastern area of Turkey and Iraq. I wouldn't sell any of these beauties." He inspected a brass pitcher before carefully sitting it on a table. "Each piece represents a different soul of my people." He touched the long scar on his forehead. "This one belonged to my aunt who passed away several years ago."

Cass turned away. Guilt. Damn guilt.

64

The bell warned them of the arrival of a new customer. Umit nodded before leaving the room. Cass inspected a small statue, thinking of her father who had a Ph.D. in English literature. When Cass, an only child, was ten he had presented her with a volume of American plays. It was already very old, so old that Cass worried she would break off the cover. Although he had barely paid any attention to her education previously, he now declared an intense interest in her studies. He wanted her collection of Judy Blume books discarded. He replaced them with Fitzgerald, Hemingway, Morrison, and Oates. He said the more intellectual British literature should be saved for when she was older. He had zero patience with commercial novels. Less for glossy-covered paperbacks. He wanted her turned into a proper literary-minded young woman who would one day write his biography.

He hired a graduate student to be her tutor. Miss Boner was sturdy, plain and plagued by allergies. It appeared there was nothing she wasn't allergic to, including ten-year-olds, especially clever little ten-year-old girls with curls. She had a nasty temper that she never showed Cass's parents and smelled like dead fish, bottom-feeding carp, to be exact.

When the sessions first started, Cass devoured the first book the night before and greeted Miss Boner with a quote from page sixty and an enthusiastic discussion of the characters. Miss Boner's eyelids had lowered ever so slightly and she began to sneeze uncontrollably, so uncontrollably that Cass was sprayed by her spit. Miss Boner was pissed at Cass. Cass didn't know why, but consequently, she never quoted word for word again. This, Cass noticed, seemed to end Miss Boner's coughing spells.

It didn't take long to realize that Miss Boner took her job way too seriously. She gave tests and if Cass didn't receive at least 90 percent she reported her to her father. At which point Cass quickly was taken into her bedroom and her father showed her again and again what happened to young girls who didn't know how to study.

"Tell your mother and you'll both pay," he always warned. "This is our secret."

It was the sexual abuse by her father that her therapist assured her had caused the most emotional and mental damage.

The sound of the bell signaled the shop door opening again. Cass brought her thoughts back to the room as Umit returned.

"The Germans left. Come, it's time to hear what's been happening in our lives." Umit's arm encircled Cass's shoulders in a fatherly way. Cass made herself not pull away. Then one-by-one, he lit candles before sitting on a cushion. She sat beside him, but placed a pillow between them and they began to talk. Their voices were low, melodious hums. The words and atmosphere of the shop wove a gossamer web that Cass wanted to resist, but found that she couldn't.

"Your old friend Justina lives in Ankara. Do you plan to visit her?"

Cass started. "Actually, I just talked with her. She, uh, has changed."

"Prison life is not a pleasant experience. It changes people."

Cass lowered her head. At times, he looked so much like her father it was uncanny, frighteningly, taking her back to places she didn't want to go. She didn't raise her head as she spoke. "I feel I must apologize for what happened. To…"

Umit raised his hand. "Justina and I have made our peace."

"I'm glad. I, uh…" Cass hesitated, continuing to look at the floor. The time was perfect for her to confess her role, but knowing what she should do and doing it were not the same things.

Minutes ticked away. Say something now. This is the time.

Cass said nothing, but she felt Umit's eyes upon her. She looked at him. When she spoke, her words had nothing to do with a confession or desire for forgiveness. They were about a memory she had never spoken of:

"Odd. I just remembered when my father kissed me for the last time. I was fourteen. We were in the backyard. I had hit a baseball hard and it went flying over the back fence. I was excited, so I ran to him. He was laughing. He pulled me close and kissed me on the lips, then he pushed me to arm's length and looked at me for the longest time. I saw an odd look come over his face and he said: 'You're becoming a woman, Cass. We won't do that again.'"

Cass glanced away, pursed her lips, and blinked fast. Would she ever be able to admit what her father had done to her to another person again? Would the feeling of shame ever go away? The therapist said when she trusted someone enough, she would be able to talk about it. When she did, it would be a step toward full mental health. Other survivors of childhood abuse talked about it freely—the news was rife with reports of child abuse—but still... She set down her cup.

"He never, ever did it, I mean that...again." Cass shot a glance at Umit. The cat jumped into his arms, circled three times, then nestled in his lap. He stroked its head. Cass kept in her sigh and shook off her morose mood, planting another smile on her face.

"We did, however, learn to shoot a gun together. We went to target practice once a week for about a year. He thought that was a proper thing for a father and teenage daughter to do. But it didn't take him long to declare I was too much of a girl to ever learn to shoot well."

Umit chuckled and rubbed the cat's ears. "I like the butterfly."

Cass touched the breast pocket that had a multi-colored butterfly embroidered on it and smiled. "Sometimes I wonder what's important," she said.

"To nurture our souls." He placed the palms of his hands together in front of his chest and bowed slightly. "You know the butterfly is the symbol of the soul or psyche I presume."

Pressing her lips together, she looked away

Cass wanted to talk freely, but she couldn't do it. She just couldn't. She had once trusted her father and mother and look what happened. She had once trusted her husband and look what happened. She had once trusted Justina and look what happened. She hadn't known Justina was a thief, not until it was too late and she too weak and entangled to free herself. Besides, once she got up the nerve to confess that she had a role in the robbery, Umit certainly would not want to be her friend. Why would she want someone who wasn't a friend know her darkest secret?

He cleared his throat. "I'm taking a carpet-buying trip to the East tomorrow. Would you like to join me? We'd be back in two days."

Hesitant, but more than curious about the eastern part of Turkey where she knew an American woman visitor was an oddity, Cass agreed. The bell rang again. Cass followed him out of the room, excused herself, and left.

Outside, she realized that she'd forgotten to ask Umit for advice about the job offer. Damn. But, there would be plenty of time to bring up that subject on the trip to eastern Turkey. She didn't need to let Timur Sahin know until next week.

She wrapped her scarf around her neck and hailed a taxi. A man flicked a lighter.

Glancing his way, she frowned.

13

Umit

After Cass left the shop, Ali came to his brother. Before they could say anything, the doorbell jingled. The man in a red shirt and leather jacket entered.   His hair and coat were bathed in new fallen snow.

"What do you have to report?" Umit asked.

"After the Griffith woman and the other American talked, Justina Ismit met with Sevgi Arslan at Arlan's apartment.   Arslan works for Yapi Kredi bank, and as you know, Ismit works for Is Bank. Something is definitely not right."

The men discussed their strategies for further surveillance before the visitor left.

Ali turned to Umit. "What have you heard from the foreign minister?"

"He's avoiding a meeting."

"Then you are concerned?"

"Yes."

Ali sighed. "Integrity is such a difficult virtue to maintain. By the way, I was surprised you showed Cass that room."

"I forgave her long ago."

"Yes, but wasn't that putting temptation in her path?"

"Only if we believe she's still a thief. I choose to believe she's changed."

"That's why you're having her followed?" Ali said with a grin.

"I'm no fool."

"And the Kurds thank you for that."

Deep in thought, they closed the shop and retired to their homes.

Stacks of articles surrounded Umit's computer. No one ever touched them. Sometimes when he felt particularly brave—or foolish, he would send off an one for publication. He would never sign his work: "Here's what I think," he would say anonymously, fearing public exposure.

When he was not writing, he would read, wanting to ground himself in a world where he could sense the touch of Allah. He read systematically, beginning at the first word, the first sentence, and going forward, skipping nothing.

He admired men like Mohammed, Gandhi, Thoreau, and Martin Luther King, but did not feel that he could live up to their example. Like them, he had suffered. From the age of seventeen to twenty-three he had spent his days and nights in a windowless isolation cell, all because of written words printed in the college newspaper. His only visitor had been a toothless jailer who brought him the food that his mother prepared.

Tired, Umit rubbed his scar as he read. Realizing what he was doing, he lowered his hand and pressed his fingers into the stack of papers on his desk. He cocked his head as he felt the floor shudder. Breathing deeply, he pressed down harder. The desk trembled. His eyes widened as the light fixture over his head swayed. The bulb blinked, went out, and came back on as the earth settled and Umit's resolve to work steadfastly for the benefit of his people deepened. People deserved safe homes. He would go to the minister's office in the morning.

Umit thought about the American. Tonight she had revealed nothing about why she had come to Turkey. He would learn soon, he was sure. He would not be surprised if Cass ended up being a disappointment, although, once again, as it had years ago, his fatherless heart reached out to her. She was still like a daughter to him. The young found it hard to keep values straight. Was Cass, the older adult, more honest? He could only hope.

Of course it was always possible that the woman had just learned more skillful, subtle ways of hiding her intentions. The trip to Diyarbakir would be, he knew, a good way to find out more about why this woman was again in Ankara.

When he was a young man, he had thought in a hallucinatory moment that he could convince those heading on the wrong path to change. But life and years had taught him that people had to find their own way, make their mistakes, and maybe even die not having found the right path. It was not possible for most strong-willed, determined people to listen to another for more than a few brief seconds without rebelling.

Cass Griffith was out of her element. If she proved herself, once again, to be an enemy of the Turkish people, she would pay dearly for her mistake. She had been lucky the first time. At their next meeting Umit would press for information. Right now, the best plan was to make sure the American trusted him and to wait for the facts to be revealed.

71

She did not know Turkish. That disadvantage would bring her to confide in Umit, of this, he was sure. She obviously thought him a fool. He would use this to advantage, this error in her thinking.

Umit snapped his book closed. The light in his eyes gleamed with determination and strength. His bones ached. He was not getting any younger. Hattice was right, they should move away from all this intrigue. Unfortunately, it could never happen, not as long as he was needed.

His wife walked into the room. He stood and pulled her close.

14

Cass

Cass's body hugged the car door as the driver revved the motor. Umit unconsciously stroked the long scar on his face, then patted a map on the seat.

"I thought you would enjoy looking at this as we travel. Personally, I love to follow a map when I go to the east. GPSs bore me."

"I seem to always travel by the seat of my pants," Cass said.

They chuckled.

"You Americans are funny creatures. You are always moving, never still."

They left Ankara with Umit pointing out spots on the map. Miles passed. Cass looked out the window. Shells of half-completed buildings were everywhere. "I'm surprised at all the development."

"You won't see this kind of building going on as we move farther east. Not much money has been allotted for that area of our country. Civil war doesn't encourage development."

"When do you think the fighting in the east will end?"

"When do you think all terrorists will be eliminated?"

In silence Cass watched the changing landscape of Anatolia, the snow-covered fields strewn with discarded papers, skeletons of unfinished houses, women bent over in gardens filling baskets with thatch. Cass started to mention that she had come to Turkey to interview as a contractor, but instead she pulled out her cigarette pack and turned to Umit, "Cigarette?"

Umit smiled, snapped his head upward and clicked his tongue against the roof of his mouth. "Quit. Doctor's orders."

Cass leaned forward and offered the driver a cigarette. He took it and put it on his ear, thanking her. Pulling up within a foot of the overloaded truck in front of them, he cut into the oncoming lane, then snapped back in front of the truck (again within a foot) and gunned the motor.

A sparkling-clean pink and lavender bus passed the overloaded truck in the same manner.

The driver glanced into the rearview mirror and stepped down on the gas pedal. Nervous? Does he seem nervous? Cass frowned and looked behind, but saw nothing suspicious.

A couple on a motorcycle sped past. Cass settled back into the seat and grinned. One of the things on her "to do" list was to buy a Harley. If she remained in Turkey, she was sure that's what she wanted. "If I stay longer in Ankara, I'd like to buy a motorcycle. Could you help me with the red tape?"

Umit chuckled. "I see why my boys thought you were a tough woman when they first saw you. Of course I would. Are you thinking of prolonging your stay?"

"Possibly."

Umit's cell phone buzzed. He answered it and spoke in rapid-fire Turkish.

In her youth Cass was a lover of roller coasters. She still was, although she hadn't ridden one in years. She coughed, flicking her cigarette butt out the window.

Umit pocketed his phone. "I see I'm not the only one who should quit smoking."

The driver steered the Mercedes into a rest stop; he scanned the parked cars before he turned off the motor.

As Umit and Cass sat at an outdoor table, Cass leaned forward on her arms. "I have a chance to work in Turkey."

Umit listened intently while Cass told him about the banker and the offer. When she said the banker's name, Umit's eyebrows arched. "I know this man."

"Great. I'd like to be part of building some sound housing here in Turkey."

"Don't make any decisions until I check things out. I'll make some calls."

15

Cass

The next day Umit and Cass again sat at a table at another roadside café. The snow had stopped falling and with the warm temperature, what remained on the ground was now melted. Seven buses filled the parking lot. Men in white shirts and dress pants laughed and talked as they sprayed the vehicles that were cleaned, inside and out, at every stop.

Cass remembered this particular roadside café as a place of overcast, cloud-covered sky and pungent air, suffused with a perpetual smell of roasting lamb on a spit. And it was exactly that. People were scattered about the tables eating bowls of rice and beans, sipping *cay* out of tulip-shaped glasses. Except for the brightness of the sun, much seemed the same as the last time Cass had rested at this very spot with another Turkish man.

At a nearby table, a young man in a black leather jacket and blue jeans reached over and cut the sliced tomato on the plate for his son. His head-scarfed wife held a sleeping baby girl in her arms. The woman's sea-foam–colored coat hung to the ground.

A vineyard grew across the highway and behind the field. Fairy chimneys, conical-shaped rock formations capped with basalt boulders, added an element of ancient mysticism to the scene. Soft grays, tans, and browns outlined a sky of the clearest blue dotted with white clouds. Beyond the erosion-formed chimneys, cavernous interiors of Mt. Erciyes whispered a history of persecution and abuse of those who wished for religious freedom.

"There's an underground city not far from here," Umit said. "Originally, they were hiding places for the early Christians. Most are now abandoned, but some are secretly in use."

Cass dropped three sugar cubes into her tea glass as she gazed at the view and remembered the day at this table when her Cappadocia friend had revealed Justina's secret.

"She's a lesbian."

"She is not!"

"She told Abdul she was."

The woman Cass had been traveling with for six months, whom she had had more than one discussion about how gays were horribly mistreated, whom she had shared rooms with, the only one she had ever been able to tell about her childhood abuse, couldn't trust her enough to tell her this important detail about her life? Cass couldn't believe it.

When she had confronted Justina, she had shrugged. Why does that matter, Justina wanted to know.

"But, you never told me. We are friends. How could you not have told me this?"

Again, Justina had shrugged. "I don't need sex in a relationship," she'd said.

All the blood had drained from Cass's face. What did that comment mean? What? Did Justina see them in a platonic relationship? Was she in love with her? Cass could understand how this could happen. A gay person could fall for a heterosexual one. But the dishonesty? No way. How could Cass trust such a woman? She could not. She left for Greece the following day. Justina robbed the shop and was arrested the next day. Not until she got professional help did Cass speak of her abuse again. The idea of trusting someone with her secret flew out the window like a feather blown by the wind.

A distant fairy chimney cast a long shadow across the thin layer of snow. Cass watched several vultures circling. She pulled her coat tighter around her now-chilled body, feeling as if by merely thinking her thoughts, she had betrayed Justina's confidence to all those at this outdoor café, but knowing she hadn't. After all, Justina had never included her as someone to share confidences with. And she had loved Justina. More than she had ever loved another person.

In a gentle voice Umit asked if she were all right.

Cass nodded and directed the conversation in a different direction. "What's Diyarbakir like? I always wanted to go to that part of Turkey, but as an American woman, never had the nerve."

Umit finished his *cay*. "Dark. Poverty stricken. A center for death and violence."

Umit's head, in shadow now, was framed by a blue sky.

The child at the next table shouted, "*Anne`, Anne`*, can I have more juice?"

Somewhere down the highway a truck whined. Someone driving against a deadline. A gray outline appeared on the highway. It moved closer without becoming clear before changing abruptly to a gray-black shadow

78

shooting past, only to vanish, swallowed up by the turn in the road. The trucker would kill himself, driving that recklessly.

Poor fool. Poor, misguided, thoughtless fool.

"It's a place where people are struggling to survive," Umit continued. "Most have lost someone close to them in the war. It's not Ankara or Istanbul; it's not a Mediterranean Sea village. It's Diyarbakir, Kara Amid, the Black Chief." Umit leaned forward. "And you, my friend, why have you returned to Turkey looking so lost? Only to work?"

Cass looked off in the distance a long time before speaking. "At home, all I do is work. When I was a kid, my mother always kept me busy. Work, work, work. My mom is a workaholic. Work, she said, was the way to keep me out of trouble. I rebelled at fifteen and left, spent years going with the flow, not buying into the system. But, uh, well, I forgot about people, about me. I guess I decided somewhere along the line those things didn't matter."

"You don't have close friends in America?"

"Not really. I haven't had time, or haven't taken the time to develop any." Cass knew it was because she couldn't bring herself to trust anyone. She glanced at Umit. Especially Umit she couldn't trust, the man who reminded her of her father. Especially not Umit. But strangely enough, it had felt good to confess this to him, something that surprised her.

The sun lowered in the sky. "If you want to change that, I'm sure you can make it happen. One just needs to look inward, to be patient, to endure, to trust. To let go of the past."

Such wise words. If she could only follow them.

Finishing their tea in silence, they stood and walked to the Mercedes. The driver separated himself from the crowd of men near the gift shop and hurried to the car. He opened the door for Umit, ran around to Cass's side, but she was already seated.

79

"We'll visit Kayseri first. There's someone there I think you should meet."

They drove over an hour without speaking. Cass pretended to sleep. She was thinking that what she had hoped for from this trip to Turkey was an instant fix. Forgiveness from two people to eliminate her soul ache. She also needed reassurance that it was okay to let the old masks she'd created since childhood die, to "pluck up" what was planted and to burn all the fragments in a wild bonfire and come out a different, better person. But how could she explain this to Umit? Cass believed her salvation would begin with Justina's forgiveness and come to completion with Umit's. Cass was sure of it. She had to be sure. But it was more than difficult to take the steps.

Umit turned to her. "Last year over ten thousand people in northern Turkey died because of the bad housing built by an ill-advised, shortsighted government and greedy men. The earthquake toppled the homes as if they were made of cardboard." His voice cracked.

Cass listened half-heartedly while gazing at her shadowy reflection in the window. She knew for years she'd been experiencing deep existential loneliness, but she hadn't known what to do about it until she'd had her therapy. For too long she had denied her inner misery by keeping obsessively busy.

Umit was talking. "It's important that doesn't happen again. You were wise to talk to me; the Turkish people's safety must be the foremost consideration."

"Yes…of course…"

The car flew past a woman in a white headscarf riding a donkey, a large bundle of cuttings from a field was strapped to the donkey's rear. Cass couldn't help but imagine her as a character in a Greek myth.

Cass's given name was Cassandra. In Greek mythology Cassandra was the daughter of King Priam and Queen Hecuba and the twin sister of Helenus. She was favored by

80

Apollo who gave her the gift of prophecy, but when she wouldn't be seduced by him, he cursed her by making sure her prophecies would never be believed. Given her childhood and ignored pleas for help as a child, Cass thought the connection was ironic. The thought darkened her mood even further. She reached for the map, unfolded it, and found their location halfway between Nevsehir and Urgup. "Which route will we follow?"

Umit leaned forward and spoke to the driver in Turkish. As the driver responded, his eyes darted from right to left. He looked behind before he glanced at his watch, and then responded to Umit who nodded and spoke.

Cass had the feeling that the men were talking about something it would be wise for her to know. Without knowing their language better, her awareness of what was happening was far too limited.

"We'll take Highway 300 to 767 then to 805. Tomorrow we will take 300 through Pinarbasi, Gurun, Maltya, Elazig, and then 885 south to Diyarbakir. That will be a much longer day. So tonight, my friend, we will relax."

Umit's cell phone buzzed. He communicated fervently in Turkish, his expression stern.

Cass was surprised and alerted by the anger she saw come and go from the usually gentle man before he hung up.

"Sorry," he said. "Just some business, nothing for you to worry about."

She was no fool. Umit was not a simple carpet dealer who collected antiquities. He was more than a father-figure whom she had once almost taken out her misplaced revenge on. He was much more. But what?

Cass blew smoke rings out the crack in the window as the landscape rushed by and she began to devise a plan to see Justina again.

16

Justina

Justina moved into the apartment just as she did everything now, quietly, numbly, her brain and soul wracked with the Ten Commandments resonating in her head. She was alone when she entered, put down her suitcases near the door, went to the living room, and sat on the flowered sofa near the window wall. She would be safe here. But, still, why didn't she just buy an air ticket and head back to the states? Why this?

She had to have time to think. The numbness would go away. How do you divorce a man when you're a foreigner in a foreign land? Could she do it across the ocean? How long would she be able to keep her job at the bank once they found out that she had been imprisoned for robbery? What if Cass called when she wasn't home and talked to Volcan?

Her hands rested on her knees, fingers spread wide. An evil eye hung from her left palm as she concentrated on breathing deeply.

Gradually she closed her fingers over her cherished token—the one thing she had kept with her from the days she and Cass spent together. Poor, darling, sweet Cass.

Taking in a breath of air, she stood and slid open the glass door, then stepped out onto the balcony. The Sheraton was only a few blocks away. A young boy walked into the small grocery store across the street. She leaned over the railing. The sidewalk, three floors below, was flanked with evergreen bushes. A round garden plot was centered within a wrought-iron fence.

She bent forward and looked up. There were at least five more floors above, something she hadn't noticed before. Was there another garden on the roof? Turks loved their gardens and rooftop terraces. Maybe there was a table and chairs. Later, after unpacking, she would go up and investigate.

Turning, she walked lethargically through the living room and dining area down the hallway to her bedroom. It was small. One window looked out onto a window of an adjoining building; the curtain was open. She pulled the cotton drapery over the glass and adjusted the pleats, carefully, making sure each pleat was folded evenly. The room would be fine while she figured out what her next move should be. Her parents were dead. Her aunt was living, but she didn't know her—would never truly know her. Her father used to say: Life was a bitch and then you die. "I see what you meant, Dad, I definitely see," she whispered as she turned from the room and walked toward her two packed bags. Her eyes were dry. Her emotions were in-check. The passageway was dim, but she didn't bother to switch on the light; the dimness held a comfort that suited her like a warm sweater.

Before she opened her bags, she sat on the bed remembering her first lover and their first night together. The older woman had caressed Justina's arm and her breasts with the softest of touches and aroused her sexuality, awaking Justina to who she always knew she was, but had denied.

Justina stood and reached for one of her bags. When she opened it, she gasped. Lying on the top of her white blouse, the last thing she remembered packing, was the pearl-handled letter opener that belonged to her boss, Osman Celik. How had it gotten into her bag? Who had put it there? Cautiously, she picked it up and set it on the dresser before returning to her unpacking. The words, "Thou shalt not steal" tripped through her head. Frantically she searched for her Bible, her stabilizer, but it was not there.

Like a zombie now, her unpacking was methodical. Occasionally she stopped, look at the opener, grimace, and return to her work.

As she pulled the last carefully folded skirt out of her bag, she glanced again at the offending knife. Reaching toward the mattress, she leaned on it for support as she sat, terrified, convinced that the Lord would punish her. A vivid picture of her mother formed in her head. Like her mother, she was obviously a natural thief. How else did her boss's letter opener get into her possession? She had taken it. "Don't let the bastards get you down," she heard with the clarity of a church bell's ring.

She felt trapped in that quiet dark moment. She had stolen, and instead of facing her husband with the truth that while she still loved him, she also loved a woman, she had secretly made plans to leave him, and she had left. She was a sinner of the highest order. She deserved the worst punishment.

Her eyes widened. Her body doubled over in pain. Her hand covered her mouth. She would burn in Hell. There would be no salvation for her. None. Not in heaven or on earth.

Perspiration dotted her forehead. She was damned, *damned,* and so like her mother.

 She did not move from the bed as dusk turned to night. When she stood, her movement was that of an exhausted, determined traveler on an electronic walkway in an airport. Without looking right or left she drifted out of the room, down the hallway and out the door, haunted.

Each step she took to the rooftop was precise, careful, orderly. So like the new Justina. It was almost as if she were being led.

As she stood on the ledge, she envisioned Cass standing beside her, holding hands, looking into each other's eyes.

"Sweet, dear Cass," Justina whispered, stepping forward into the crisp, welcoming night air.

Murmurings. Shocked eyes. Crunching snow.

With her final breath, Justina's fingers unclasped and the evil eye rolled into the frozen flowerbed.

17

Cass

In Kayseri the driver steered through deserted streets then veered down a narrow alleyway. Stopping in front of a building, he got out and running around the car, opened Umit's door. Two men in suits came forward. The driver nodded at them and his shoulders seemed to relax. Cass looked right to left, then tossed her cigarette into a dark corner.

Something was up, something sinister. In the states she carried a concealed pistol. She wished she'd been able to bring it with her.

Umit spoke to the men in Turkish as two smiling girls dressed in royal-blue school uniforms ran out of the side doorway. The young girls giggled as they hugged Umit and were introduced to Cass who was told she was the first American they had ever met.

Taking Umit's arms, the girls hurried up two flights of stairs. When the older woman wearing a headscarf, apparently the girls' mother, saw Cass, she switched immediately into broken English.

Umit raised his eyebrows in a wordless question.

"He's sleeping."

Umit nodded.

Pakize motioned to the girls. They scurried away.

As the adults sat on the old-fashioned overstuffed sofa, the girls, Ayse and Gul, arrived with a round enamel tray of partially filled tea glasses and a plate of baklava and biscuits. Their hair, thick and dark. Their skin, clear and smooth as finely sanded pieces of oak. Ayse poured hot water from the pot.

Smiling broadly, the girls stared at Cass. Pakize raised her eyebrows. They lowered their heads and backed away.

"Will you stay for supper?" Pakize asked.

"No, we have reservations at the Hotel Capari. But, thank you. Next time I'm through I will," Umit promised.

He looked at Cass. "Excuse our rudeness for a minute." He shifted toward Pakize and spoke in Turkish while Cass surveyed the room, attempting to pick up some of what he was saying.

Several pictures of the girls at different ages hung on the wall above a table holding a boom box and a Koran on a crocheted white scarf. A frayed and faded Persian carpet covered the wood floor. Glass doors separated one room from another.

The only word Cass caught was the Turkish word for thank you.

When Pakize and Umit stopped speaking, Pakize glanced at Cass shyly, smiled, and said to the girls, "Bring your uncle."

They left.

Cass caught sight of a blue evil eye. Her thoughts shifted away from the room to her recent conversation with Justina at the café. If only she had spoken up. If only she hadn't been so hesitant.

A short, thin elderly man with twinkling eyes now stood in the doorway. To Cass's surprise, he wore a cream-colored robe and a tall, conical hat—the clothing of a dervish.

Umit rose, walked to the older man's side, kissed his hand and touched it with his forehead. They spoke in Turkish.

"Umit Bey is such a good man," Pakize said. "Without his help my daughters would not be able to afford the education they are receiving. He is a good, good man," she said warmly, beaming at the men's backs. "We still have not heard where my husband is; he disappeared…" Her eyes moistened. She did not finish her sentence.

Cass didn't know what to say, so instead she patted the woman's shoulder. The girls averted their eyes. Cass glanced at Umit who nodded at her. The elderly man walked over and took her shoulders, welcoming her into his home. Then he spoke to the girls, and they went to the boom box.

Gul pushed the "On" button, then leaned back against the wall next to her sister. The man raised his arms and as if frozen in a layer of thin ice, waited. The palm of one hand pointed upward, the other down. One minute. Two. Three. The music began slowly, quietly like a gentle winter breeze. In rhythm with the hypnotic beat, the dervish began to turn. His swirling graceful. His head bent to the left. As the rhythm quickened, so did the dervish.

Cass leaned her head back on the sofa and half-closed her eyes as the old man continued to twirl. Like a weaver of fine bamboo thread, he spun her into a dream-like state. The words "Everything is coming to me easily and effortlessly" went through her head. It was as if she were meditating. She felt as if she were sinking into herself. Deeper and deeper and deeper.

In her mind's eye, a white wolf came toward her. Clear eyed, thick furred, nostrils close to her face.

The tape clicked off. When Cass raised her eyelids, the feeling of being deep inside herself remained. The dervish stopped spinning and lowered his hands, his arms and then his head.

Through a layer of emotional fog Cass blinked. The dervish put palm to palm and bowed.

Cass had the strange, overpowering and sure feeling she had been visited by her spiritual guide, the wolf. A guide who would always be present to protect her.

Umit and Pakize leaned close together and spoke softly for several minutes in Turkish while Cass settled back into reality.

Glancing at his watch, Umit stood and placed his hand on Cass's arm. "We must be going."

"Oh, please! We must have a picture first!" Gul said.

Umit laughed, grabbed the nearest girl and hugged her.

After the picture taking, when Cass, a woman who hated to stand in front of a camera, had smiled through several shots, they walked to the door. Umit repeated his promise to stay for dinner the next time he traveled through. The old man spoke to Umit in Turkish. Then placing his hands on Cass's shoulders, he peered straight into her eyes and said word to her she could not understand. When he was through, Umit translated.

"This is what he said: I hope you'll understand what I'm telling you. I hope you'll hear it all the way to your little toenails. You must learn to be still—to wait. When you are waiting you're not doing nothing. You're doing the most important something there is. You're allowing your soul to grow up. When you feel soul ache, if you can't be still and wait, you can't become what Allah created you to be."

The dervish held Cass's shoulders until Umit stopped translating. When he released them, he bowed with his palm across his heart. Charmed, Cass did the same.

Later in the car, Umit spoke softly, "Years ago, before the originator of our republic, Ataturk, forbid it, their uncle practiced the life of a dervish. Sufism is a mystical religious sect that welcomes all to its beliefs. He later became a *hoca*, a village priest. He has been to Mecca five times. He is a seer, a man of great ancient wisdom, a mystic. He says you have an old soul," Umit said, "and thinks you belong in Turkey."

"When you speak to him next, tell him his comments honor me."

Later, after settling in their rooms at the hotel, Umit and Cass ate dinner in the hotel restaurant and bar.

A stained-glass window bled a brilliant puddle on the floor. Another large evil eye hung on the wall near their table. As they sipped on their glasses of raki, a group of Turkish musicians dressed in bright red, gold, and blue costumes began to set up their equipment.

"There's a fine woman dancer here." Umit glanced around the room. His expression darkened. He set down his glass.

Cass frowned and turned to see what had caused the sudden change in Umit's demeanor.

Three men sat at the far end of the room. The two older ones were robust, distinguished looking; one wore a turban wrapped around his head. Cass recognized the third man. He was middle-aged, thinner, but expensively dressed—the bank manager who had interviewed her, Timur Sahin. He saw them and excusing himself, sauntered toward their table.

"Umit Bey, such a surprise to see you. How is my father's old friend? And Cass Griffith, what a surprise. I didn't know you had friends in Turkey."

"Cass and I have known each other for years," Umit said. "Strange company you're keeping."

Timur chuckled.

Umit leaned toward Cass. "My apologies. We need to speak in Turkish for a moment."

Cass raised her hand in a "not a problem" motion, sipped her drink, and told herself she was taking a Turkish language course as soon as possible.

Umit spoke in a warning tone. Timur's voice was bemused. He laughed and switched back to English. "I am no longer a boy, Umit Bey. Trust me to be able to take care of myself." He turned his attention to Cass. "I look forward to our next meeting."

As he walked away, a growl slipped from Umit's lips. "That is a foolish man," he said. "Excuse me. I'll be right back." He headed for the lobby.

Music vibrated. Men began to sing. Cass couldn't help but notice that she was the only woman in the room.

Umit returned. "Like everywhere in the world, there are people in Turkey who are so greedy and evil that they are willing to sacrifice the lives of many for their own purpose."

Across the room, Timur was talking and gesturing.

Cass nodded toward the table. "And he may be one of them?"

"Unfortunately, it's possible."

The musicians changed songs.

A woman with gyrating hips whirled into the room. Her voluptuous breasts and full body were barely covered in a shimmering blue and green garment with gold sequins. The men's fingers tapped and snapped in time with the music, as she moved among the tables, at times bringing her breasts close to their faces. The men licked their lips and stuffed lira into her sequined bra.

Three men jettisoned out of their seats and raising their hands joined her. Hips met; her belly rippled. Faster. Faster. The men called out in ecstasy and the woman backed away with a sultry smile as the music slowed and then ended. The men collapsed and sprawled on the floor to the laughter of the crowd.

The far table was now empty. The dancer was gone. The room soon lay in a bed of sweaty silence.

Cass stood. "I'll be off. Thanks for the evening. See you at breakfast. Goodnight."

Lying in bed, Cass listened to an eastern gale howl as she wrote in her journal. Writing like this made her go inward, making her feel as if she had wings. Not thinking about anything in particular, she began to write a description of the dervish: his white gown, conical hat, the music, the smell of sweat and jasmine, his trance-like expression. She recalled his words: learn to be still. Words that to her translated to action through non-action. But wasn't that her problem? She couldn't overcome her urge to run from the truth.

She put down her pencil and notebook, stretched out on the bed, gazing at the white wolf in her mind.

18

Umit

In his room Umit was talking on his phone to his brother. "He sent a document to the Black Sea concerning the proposed government-backed housing project via Sevgi Arslan? Damn. And Timur is here with one of the Ankara police academy chiefs and that gangster, Abdullah Kaya."

Ali exclaimed and Umit continued. "Find out all you can," he said, closing the phone.

Unbuttoning his shirt, Umit unsnapped the bulletproof vest that Hattice insisted he wear. Often he worried that he had let his people down by not being a public figure. This was a recurring conversation with his brother and wife. They both told him he was doing the right thing. But he knew the only thing holding him back from going public was his own fear. Fear he had never been able to overcome. He went to the window.

Moonlight cast shadows on the distant minaret. A lone figure dashed across the street and disappeared in an alley. A cat screamed. Although his room was well heated, Umit shivered.

19

Cass

The muddy Tigris River flowed with a strange familiarity that made her spine itch. An angler fished on the bank. On a blanket, not far away, a woman in a headscarf prepared what appeared to be tea on a portable burner. Something wasn't right. Cass could feel it. But the open-air café built under a large tree was quiet and cool. A Turkish couple relaxed at a table near the kitchen, chatting in low tones. By appearances, the day was peaceful, even sublime. Cass knew different.

"I'd love to have a cigarette," Umit said as he sipped his sugar-laced tea.

Surprised, Cass reached for her pack.

Umit raised his hand. "Would love to, but won't," he said. "You should quit."

"Yeah, yeah." She blew smoke to the side. "Why is it all smokers who quit become born-again preachers?"

With a look of grotesque anguish, Umit stood. "Forgive..." and then, abruptly, he sat again, grabbing for his chest.

The driver darted to the table and pulled a bottle of pills from his pocket. Opening it, he put one into Umit's mouth and raised a glass of water to his lips. Umit closed his eyes. The driver shot an irritated look at Cass before bowing his head and stepping back two steps.

"Are you okay?" Cass asked.

Umit's eyes remained half-closed. "Just the old heart," he said softly. "The doctor says I have many years ahead of me. It's just that sometimes I forget to take my medication. Come, the city awaits us."

Cass had no idea. If she had known, she wouldn't have smoked in the car. Dammit. Concerned, she stayed close to him as they headed toward the driver who was waiting near the opened back door.

She ran around the back, kicked a can out of her path, slid inside and leaned her head back on the seat. Turkish music at low volume filled the car's interior. Cass was reminded again of the dervish's spiritual dance. Be still, wait. Wait? Where did waiting get anyone?

In what seemed to be no time at all, a high prison-like wall came into sight. Cass thought of how Justina had been incarcerated for years. The rats. The endless hours. She shuddered inwardly.

After passing through an opening in the twelve-meter high Byzantine fortification, they turned left and wove through a maze of narrow, twisting, unmarked streets. Black basalt houses flanked each side. Dark-skinned men walked arm-in-arm. A bridled horse stood outside of a shop, munching grain from a basket attached to its head. A stooped man in a suit with a large wooden cage full of chickens strapped to his back stumbled, then straightened and continued on. A colorfully painted wagon filled with old machine parts lumbered by. The scene was picturesque in a Gothic sort of way.

"This is the place," Umit said.

The car stopped in front of a flower shop.

The driver spoke in a respectful tone to Umit.

"Yes, I'm fine," Umit said in English. "We'll go in."

When Umit and Cass walked inside, a man behind the counter looked up, rushed over and bowed to Umit before glancing furtively at the clock on the wall. Nodding to Cass, he motioned for them to follow.

Sensing urgency and danger, Cass frowned as they weaved through the rooms, climbed a flight of stairs and entered the man's home. A gloomy energy permeated the building. She sat on the edge of a chair.

From another room a younger man carried out a wooden chest and set it in front of Umit. He was apparently the son of the shop owner. Same nose. Same eyes. First, he withdrew an exquisitely woven silk *kilim* in shades of brown and gold. Umit admired it and then gave a price. The owner jerked his head upward and made a customary clicking sound, meaning no. Umit named another price. The older man shot a look at the young man who once again bent over the chest.

Cass was facing Umit's back. Her stomach was churning like a broken washing machine. Unable to sit any longer, she stood and went to the window. A man maneuvered a horse-drawn wagon down the street. A woman in a black, billowing *chador* scurried into a building. Nervous, Cass tapped her shoe on the wooden floor.

The wall shelf was covered with a crocheted doily. There must be a woman in this house somewhere. Where was she? Where was the customary offer of tea? Cass heard no sounds coming from the kitchen or anywhere else in the house. Odd, very odd. The shopkeeper's movements were

97

quick, hurried and fretful. He knocked into his son. "*Tamam, tamam*," he said.

Umit frowned.

The man ducked his head and handed over the *kilim* and a woven donkey bag. Taking a bulging envelope from Umit, he kissed his hand, then nodded to his son who shot a glance to the window.

Umit spoke sharply to the shopkeeper, who threw up his hands, gesturing for them to leave.

"Don't know what's going on," Umit said, "but hurry." He took the steps two at a time. So did Cass. The sound of the heavy door slamming behind them echoed down the silent, deserted street.

Umit spoke to the driver as they jumped in. The driver pressed the gas pedal and the car shot away. In the next instant, they jerked to the left missing a vegetable cart. Cass gasped and grabbed the back of the front seat.

Boom! Cass screamed. Debris sprayed high into the air. Glass, shattered wood and metal showered down on the Mercedes as it sped around the corner. An army truck, seemingly coming from nowhere, roared toward them.

"On the floor."

Cass folded herself between the driver's seat and the back seat. Umit was close enough to smell his sweat.

"Now, pray."

Out of the corner of her eye, Cass looked at Umit's deep scar. She had never asked him where he had gotten it. Now she didn't want to know. She grit her teeth as the car jerked to the right, then to the left. She bent lower as the car swerved dangerously, balancing precariously on two wheels before righting itself and speeding away. Wait, my foot! Shit!

The car sped forward, careening from one side of the highway to the other, occasionally dropping off the pavement. Cass could tell that Umit was praying and she hoped his prayers were for all three of them, because she had no faith her prayers were ever answered.

The driver mumbled and Unit touched the top of her head and retook his seat. The car slowed. Cass pushed herself up from the floor.

"I'll take a cigarette now." Umit held out his hand.

With a trembling hand, Cass reached into her pocket and pulled out her pack. Umit took one. The driver, another. She lit them.

"That was quite a thrill, huh?" Umit said.

"Like riding a roller coaster out of control. How's your heart?"

He inhaled deeply.

Cass eyed him, and thought again about her now deceased father. How would he have reacted in this situation? Easy. He would never have been in Turkey in the first place. Going to a developing country would never interest him, not even on a tour. He would be afraid of the water, the food, the culture, of the fact he couldn't speak the language. And he most certainly would not be someone who would financially help children, especially foreign girls, get a higher education.

Umit's phone buzzed. He pulled it out of his jacket, turned his head toward the door and spoke in a steady, low voice.

Cass tapped her cigarette on the edge of the rolled-down window and blew out a puff of smoke. It blew back into her face. She coughed and pushed the button on the door handle. The window slowly rose.

Umit ended the call, lowered his window and tossed out his half-smoked cigarette. Cass looked at hers, thought of Umit's heart and flicked it out as well.

"Patches work well," he said.

The car swerved to miss a donkey crossing the road. The driver stuck his head out the window and yelled.

Umit laughed. Still grinning, he leaned toward Cass and held out his left hand. Cass looked at the string of amber prayer beads and then into his eyes.

The man was a damn saint and once she had almost been part of a scheme to rob him. Well, the truth was, she *had* been part of it. She had just disappeared before it had occurred. That didn't make her any less guilty.

A finely sharpened knife blade of guilt stabbed at her heart. She needed to tell him what her part in the theft had been.

She looked into his eyes, but all she saw was her father. Biting down on her lower lip, she turned her head away.

Dammit.

She was a coward. Doing work that mostly only men did, traveling to places that most women didn't travel to, didn't mean you were brave. Brave people did not hide in a world of silence.

20

Cass

Awakening in her clothes, feeling thankful to be alive, Cass walked to the kitchen and placed two eggs into a white porcelain pan of water and lit the flame.

When the water came to a boil, she switched off the burner and dumped the eggs into a plastic colander. Picking up the salt shaker, she shook it. Empty. She grimaced, frowned at the eggs, went to the window and saw that the kiosk across the street was closed. "Well, Cassandra, you can either eat these without any salt, or you can go upstairs and knock on the door of that Turkish woman you saw in the hallway and ask to borrow some. Now, which is the best option?" she asked herself. "Duh…"

She left the apartment and climbed the stairs, tapping lightly on the door. Within seconds, she heard footsteps.

The door remained closed. "Yes?"

"Uh, hi, it's Cass from downstairs. I'm an American. I need some salt and well, the kiosk is closed. Do you mind?"

The door opened.

The woman's face was pale. She did not smile. Her eyes were red and swollen. "Hi, I'm Sevgi Arslan," she said.

"Are you okay? You look upset."

"You haven't heard?"

"Haven't heard?"

"About the suicide."

"I've been out of town. Oh, dear, surely, not your room..."

"Not, not Birkin, no, thank goodness. But a woman who had just agreed to be a roommate. She brought her bags here, walked up to the roof and jumped. It's all too horrible. We didn't really know her, but it is such a terrible thing to have happen in our building, in anyone's building really."

"How dreadful."

"It turns out she was married and pregnant, a terrible thing. Just terrible. Americans are so impulsive. Here, just a minute and I'll get you the salt." She held out her hand.

I handed her the container. "An American, you say?"

"Yes," she said over her shoulder. "Ismit. Justina Ismit. She was married to a Turk."

Ohhh! Cass grabbed for the doorframe.

The woman turned around. "Are you all right?"

Cass's body wavered.

"It can't be. Not Justina."

"Oh, dear." Sevgi moved quickly forward and took Cass's arm. "Here, come in. Sit down. I'm so sorry. I didn't realize you knew her. Dear, dear. And to hear it like that!" she said, guiding Cass into her apartment.

Cass allowed herself to be led as a wave of nausea crept up her throat. Hesitating, she bent forward and placed a hand on either side of her nose. "Oh, God!"

21

Cass

A haunting, melancholy gust of wind wafted into the room, making the curtains flutter like the wings of a hummingbird. Could it really be that Justina had moved into the same building where she now lived, climbed to the roof, and jumped to her death? The thought was just too much to accept. Cass gasped back tears, slid off the mattress, and went to the bathroom. Picking up a bottle, she took two sleeping pills and returned to the comfort of her bed.

Soon she was dreaming, floating on a cloud. An airplane made of glass came toward her from the distant horizon, a two-engine Navion beauty. Justina was the pilot, looking as she had their first time in Turkey. Long chestnut hair. Rolled-up jeans. Hiking boots. As the plane hovered over Cass a rope ladder came down from the tail. She reached up and grabbed onto the bottom rung. Higher and higher they flew until Justina's smile disappeared and Cass's fingers loosened and she fell.

In the next instant, her dream transformed. She was lying in a green field. Each part of her body was separated from the other. Standing nearby, with a saw in his hand, was the elderly man in a long white robe and cone-shaped hat from Kayseri. The dervish set the saw down and the sounds of distant music drifted across her head, her arms, her torso, legs and feet. She felt peaceful. Gently and slowly he danced and twirled around the field picking up each body part. By the end of the twirling, she was reassembled and whole again and the images evaporated like late-morning smog.

Cass awoke with a start to the ring of the telephone.

It was Umit. Her voice was thick with drugged sleep. "Umit? Did you hear about…about Justina?"

"Yes, I heard. A terrible tragedy. I'm so sorry. And unfortunately, I've got more bad news."

Cass was now sitting on the edge of the bed watching the windswept snow. "Go ahead."

"You don't want to take that job. That is, unless you don't mind being involved in the potential deaths of thousands."

"What?"

"It was good you contacted me. This whole scheme is dangerous. Go home." He hung up.

Accepting his advice without question, Cass found the bank manager's phone number on her contact list. A woman answered. "Hello, this is Cass Griffith. I had a job interview earlier in the week. Would you tell your boss that I've decided to decline the offer?"

"Why, of course. Would you like me to have him call you?"

"I have no need to talk to him. Just tell him I've made other job arrangements. Goodbye."

22

Umit

Hattice stood in the kitchen waiting for water to boil for tea. Their cell phone buzzed. She picked it up and greeted Ali: "He's sleeping. He's not feeling well. Oh, wait, here he is." She handed Umit the phone.

Ali was speaking rapidly. "They just got into a car for a meeting. It's worse than we thought."

Umit turned away from his wife. "Who's in the car?"

"Besides the driver, Celik, Sahin, Kaya, and a woman. What should we do?"

"We have to stop…" Umit grabbed his heart and leaned on the counter. The phone fell to the floor.

With an exclamation of alarm, Hattice rushed to her husband's side. Supporting him, she helped him to a chair.

Running back, she picked up the phone. "Ali, he's collapsed. I need to call an ambulance. Do what you have to do."

Umit groaned his protest but was unable to speak.

23

Umit

Umit's stay in the hospital was only for one night. His medication dosage was increased and he was warned to stay away from stress. Words that made Umit chuckle and almost brought Hattice to tears. He had returned to his shop within an hour of being discharged. Hattice promised to keep the door locked and to remain in their home away from the windows.

Stopping in front of a table, Umit grabbed the offending newspaper from a table and read the headline: *Death on the Highway Uncovers Housing Scandal.* His eyes narrowed as he scanned the article, stopped at the end and read: "Why was a member of parliament, a police academy chief, and a bank manager in the same car with a suspected member of the mafia?"

Corruption, of course. There was no other answer. And it had to do with housing in the east. Such was the speculation.

Thousands had died when poorly built homes and schools had crumbled in the last quake.

The sound of a rock striking the stone building reminded him of his rebellious youth when he had protested with his political fellow students. His friends had jokingly called him *Gazi*, the Turkish name for great leader. A folded copy of the newspaper article that had caused his arrest lay folded and yellowed in his wallet. He'd believed in the power of words. He'd believed in the triumph of the human spirit over adversity. Ataturk was his hero. Yet, for years he kept his role as a leader hidden.

Another rock hit the building.

He had devoured every book about Ataturk he could find. The library had an impressive collection. It was a joy to sit at a table and read; often he stayed until closing. He and his roommate had studied every shelved volume on Ataturk that first semester. It was a contest. He had won. That is, he had won until he began to write and publish what he thought; that if Ataturk had lived longer, he would have taken away much of the military's power and given it to the people where it belonged. He had been so young and naïve then, so full of idealism and desire to speak out.

Outside, a woman shrieked. A man shouted.

Umit groaned. He hated himself for hiding in his darkened shop. He hated himself for not being on the streets with his people, but he was unable to open the door and step out.

A bullet whizzed through the air, striking the side of the shop, shattering stone.

Umit's head snapped up when he heard the key turning in the lock of the front door, then the familiar click of his younger brother Ali's shoes on the wooden plank floor. A cold breeze swept through the room and chilled his body.

108

He pulled the angora sweater his wife had knitted him across his bulging stomach and buttoned the three buttons.

"I'm in here." He shook his head and walked to the door.

Running his fingers through his thick hair, Ali inhaled deeply but would not meet his brother's eye. Beads of ice coated his mustache. He nervously turned his cap in his hand; his head hung low.

"How are they?" Umit asked, rubbing his fingers together.

"Safe. Don't worry."

Umit poured raki out of a bottle, added water. He handed it to Ali, then went and stood in front of the darkened shop window that was now totally covered in corrugated metal.

The window vibrated. Umit turned and paced the room.

"What was it you said to him?" Umit asked.

"I told him to stop them."

"You didn't order him to kill them?"

"Of course not. I would never do that."

"But he forced the car off the road?"

Ali's hand went to his throat. His face paled.

"He couldn't have known the car would overturn. That it would catch fire."

Ali shook his head.

"Are you absolutely sure that you meant no harm to come to those people?"

"Absolutely."

Umit nodded, but he could not meet his brother's eyes. "Damn the military," he said. "Marching is *not* an act of treason. They want only justice. They have a right to protest. They know those men should not have been together in that car. The military needs to give the people a chance to have a voice without reprisal. They are not planning a coup." Abruptly he sat and dropped his head between his knees.

Shouts and the sound of thundering metal cracking stones penetrated the thick walls. Feverish voices grew louder. "Enough! Enough!"

"You'll figure out something. I know you will," Ali said.

Umit knew that his brother accepted in blind faith that he would come up with an idea to stop the protest. He bowed his head again, squinted at the pattern in the carpet, trying not to think about the weight of responsibility he felt. Vivid images came: a female statue, an olive tree, and their father's profile. He felt nothing but heaviness and numbness in his heart.

There was no immediate solution, except: one must do the best one could do at any given moment. What was the best that he could do right now?

Anguished, Umit leaned against the shelf filled with folded flat weaves and pressed his hands against the sides of his head.

"It's a joke, isn't it? Integrity? Such a childhood fantasy word."

"Just don't do anything foolish," Ali said.

Lost in his thoughts, Umit gazed at the one hundred-year-old carpet hanging on the wall. It had belonged to their father and his father before him—men of honesty and integrity.

"Those people in the car brought shame to their families, to the people of Turkey," Ali mumbled.

All at once Umit remembered: He and his father were in the mosque. His father was angry at him for a foolish act he had committed. He stood in front of him, white haired and glaring. Though his arms were thin and his face was gaunt, he looked strong to Umit's child-eyes. When their gaze met, his father raised his arms upward and told him that if a deed done was for the sake of Allah, then it was a sanctioned deed. He explained that the Islamic woman and man must remain pure, but were certainly not meant to be a chattel. He told him that one must never lie. One must be true to who one was. "Pray for answers," he said.

"You are my best student," his father added. "Even now, the other children respect and follow you."

"Always live and enforce the ways of Islam. Be true to yourself," were the last words he spoke to Umit.

Others thought Umit was strong. He knew he was weak.

Minutes ticked away. The shouting in the streets became fainter. The crowd was moving away. A gunshot rang out.

"Allah's will." There was a catch in Umit's breath, a lump in his throat. "Allah's will," he repeated, looking steadily at his brother, but seeing his father.

Ali shot to his feet and began to pace like a caged cheetah.

A tank rumbled past. Ali grew gradually but steadily more excited. Like a haunted man, he clutched and beat his fists against his pants leg. Then just as quickly, he stopped pacing to pound a tabletop. He lifted the glass, put it down untouched, and firmly ground one hand into the palm of the other.

Umit opened his mouth to speak, but changed his mind and closed it again.

Ali caught his brother's arm and clung to him, not shouting but in a begging tone. "I did the right thing. Say it, I did the right…" His voice trailed away.

Umit straightened his shoulders. "The important thing for us to agree on is this: that *we* did the right thing; *we* must accept the responsibility of this action jointly. But something must be done soon before there are more deaths. I will think of something."

Ali's shoulders visibly relaxed. The street quieted. The marching, angry people, the tanks, and the soldiers were now out of earshot.

The resulting silence was deafening.

111

Moments later, with assurances that he would be careful, Ali left the shop.

Leaning his head against the cool glass of the window, Umit let the tears he suppressed in front of his brother flow.

Umit remembered Ali when he was a young boy. His younger brother had followed him around—far too closely—like a pet at his heels. When he sat under a tree and read, Ali stretched out at his side and stared upward.

Umit placed his arms under his head and tried to imagine what Ali saw. The Russian Tolstoy called the attempt to see the world through other eyes a "spiritual experience" that most men did not bother to pursue.

On that day long ago, the pale green leaves of the willow draped the velvet carpet of grass. A field of orange poppies swayed in the breeze. A starling warbled in the branch over their heads. Clouds of cotton patterned the baby-blue sky.

"I see a dragon." Umit said, watching Ali's reaction from the corner of his eye.

"Where?"

Umit pointed. "Over there, beyond the treetops."

Ali squinted and raised up on his elbow. "I can't see it."

Umit saw Ali's blank expression. Felt his frustration. He peered into the sky once more, and then again at Ali who was squinting. Umit lowered his head. "It's gone," he said. "Don't worry. It wasn't important."

"That's not fair," Ali whined. "I never see anything in the clouds."

Umit left the shop, and hunching his shoulders, headed for home. Ali had been right. Much about life wasn't fair. We can try all we want to attempt to make things fair. We can plan and plan, draw up an outline, but in the end all we can do is sit back and watch life happen. "Not this time," Umit vowed. Not this time.

The wind lashed his body. Not far up the corridor, a solemn-faced soldier leaned in a darkened doorway, a machine-gun draped across his arm. Umit averted his eyes, studying the ground as he strolled down the faintly lit arcade where shadows loomed at every turn.

His Ottoman house was stone with exposed natural rough-hewn timbers. At the entrance, he leaned back against the wall and gazed at the clear sky. Stars glittered like diamonds spread out on a navy-blue cloth under a spotlight. In the far distance, a shooting meteor cascaded downward, fading away into the night like the rays of a flashlight with a failing battery.

His hands shook as he bent down and picked up a crushed plastic bottle buried in the tracks left by the army tanks. A stream of blood streaked the snow. He looked away and put his key in the door.

The house was quiet. He slipped off his shoes, walked to his favorite chair and collapsed onto the cushion. The smell of freshly baked bread drifted from the kitchen.

Sweet Hattice. Sweet, sweet woman.

His old walnut desk with glassed-in bookcases to the right provided a mini-sanctuary. A book sat on the smooth surface. Switching on the Tiffany lamp, he opened the cover and began to read.

Hours melted away as the pages turned.

"I am a Christian and a Hindu and a Moslem and a Jew," he said aloud, nodding his head. He stared into space, questioning: What can I do to get the people off the streets?

He frowned, shook his head, leaned toward the pages and concentrated.

"Truth, love," he whispered. "Service, scrupulous methods, no hurting by deed or word."

"But how? How then do you stop people bent on destruction? How do you protest against injustice and get results without bloodshed?" he asked himself. He turned back to the book.

"Turn the searchlight inward...perhaps the fault is partly yours," he read, knowing what he did not want to know— that the words held truth.

He looked up. The bedroom light flicked off and on, his wife's signal that she wanted him to come to bed.

Soon, my love, soon.

He set the book down and picked up a collection of essays he had been reading. "Accept the place the Divine Providence has found for you, the society of your contemporaries, and the connection of events." He clutched the book until his knuckles turned white.

He had never told anyone about the day that had started as every other, with the click of the turning lock. Although before this he had managed to remain away from the jailer, on this day, the man brought him breakfast. He supposed that it simply meant that the man hated to see him reading the Christian Bible his wife had sneaked into his cell. To the illiterate jailer, any book besides the Koran was impure; anything from the Western world would be a threat to his fundamentalist religious upbringing. This was a dangerous man, this prison guard.

And he had seen. Umit knew the man had seen.

That night at midnight his door clacked open. Umit braced himself. One guard held him down and covered his mouth. The other cursed him and raised the knife. Not once did Umit scream as the flesh of his face opened.

Even now, Umit could see the determined, hateful glint of the men's eyes, their steely shine.

Slowly, he traced his scar and pressed deep into the crevice. All these years, the men's act had controlled his life.

Umit ran his finger over the spine of the book and it stopped at the author's name. He rubbed the individual letters that formed "Emerson" back and forth, as if by doing so he would absorb them onto his very soul: Trust thyself...Trust thyself...

The lights were flipped off and on again. Hattice, his Turkish goddess, was impatient. His hand stopped its movement. His gaze drifted toward the bedroom. He looked out the window, seeing and smelling the horrors of the dark, rat-infested cell.

After the men had left, he spent two weeks in the prison hospital. Later, in his cage, day after day he had sat on his cot and done breathing and body exercises, watching the cockroaches scurry across the floor. Despite his efforts, he had become thin and weak. Through it all, he had never spoken again in prison. Silence became a badge of strength, had even helped make him a strong secret leader.

Tracing the scar, he stood and paced, crossing and re-crossing the room like a man possessed. A deep inner rumble started low in his belly. He continued to pace. His face was pale. His heart heavy. His mind locked in the past, struggling to get back to the present, so he could see a future.

As a young boy, freedom meant that all human lives were interrelated and governed by Allah. Everything that took place on earth, also took place in another spiritual plane.

The light blinked off and on again. He stopped mid-step, blinked, stared at the Tiffany lamp, sighed, bent over and switched it off. Turning toward the bedroom, his hand over his heart, he went to his wife. Loving her more than his own scarred flesh, he slid into bed. Her body moved across the sheet and molded against him like a warm pat of butter.

With Hattice's loving touch, a sharp sensation of primal pain thrust him forward into a fetal position. His body coiled like a spring and he was back in the cell again. But this time he opened his mouth and wailed, again and again and again; howling as deeply and as completely as Edward Munch's stark man.

His wife, refusing to let go, held him. She held him through the screams. Held him through the wracking sobs. Held him until his head rested, exhausted, on her shoulder.

115

She held him because she knew that sometimes holding your suffering loved ones is the best and only thing you can do.

And he confessed his secret, finally. And she listened. And she held him.

When his eyes closed and his fingers relaxed on the large brown orb encircling her hardened nipple, he felt her lay her hand on his chest to feel the rhythm of his heart. She turned off the light. It was 4 a.m.

And Umit knew what he must do.

24

Cass

Justina was dead and would be flown back to the states for her funeral. Cass had never been able to tell Justina that her decision to leave before the robbery perhaps had something to do with being homophobic. Not 100 percent. Not even a percentage high enough that Cass, at the time, recognized it as what it was. Perhaps Justina had. Cass was so young and naïve then, so unworldly. Over the years she had learned the importance of accepting who she was while trying to understand why she was who she was. Being raised in a conservative environment with a father and mother who held narrow views had cemented certain inhuman values that took much living to erase. Cass had wanted to explain this to her friend, to confess her realization, but now that would never happen. On that day long ago, Cass had needed more time to think, to process her feelings, but instead, she had run.

As she always had done.

Comfort. Forgiveness. Rebonding. The absence of loneliness. All things that would never be.

She spent the afternoon lying on the bed, staring at the ceiling or at the snow, mourning her friend, the loss of Justina's unborn child, worrying that seeing her again had been a factor in pushing Justina over the edge.

After dusk, Cass roamed Ankara, torn about what to do next, anxious because she felt she knew what needed to be done, but fearing she didn't have the strength to do it. She stepped around a couple and turned the corner. Ataturk Boulevard, a street she traveled often on her walks around the city, now looked like a hurricane-ravaged sea.

"Dammit," she mumbled, turning around to retrace her steps. But the street and sidewalk she had just come down were also filled with marchers waving signs. She'd been warned more than once to stay away from such gatherings in Turkey. And here she was in the middle of one. Listening to other's warnings wasn't one of her strengths.

Ducking her head, she maneuvered through furious people determined to move forward, looking for the first place where she could get to safety. All around her, the throng shouted. She felt smothered and vulnerable. And just like in the states, even in this mass of thousands, she felt alone.

Coming to Ankara had been a mistake. She'd accomplished nothing. And now this.

"Hey, American, stay put!"

Feeling panic rising, she glanced in the direction of the voice. The Turkish woman with chestnut hair signaled for her to wait and started her way. Sevgi, the person who had just given her the horrible news. Sevgi, the person who lived in the same apartment building. Sevgi Arslan, the last person Cass wanted to see right now.

118

But fighting the urge to hurry away, she held her position. She'd experienced a stampede of humanity before—at the end of a soccer game in England when drunken fans became overexcited by victory. Five people were killed that day while she had remained in her seat watching the onslaught of screaming men and women. Fingers clasped into fists, she glanced right to left, waiting.

Sevgi now stood shoulder-to-shoulder with her, but still she had to raise her voice so that Cass could hear. "You shouldn't be here!"

Like Cass, the Turkish woman wore a short wool jacket with large buttons, a black and white hat that looked like a helmet, blue jeans, and flat-heeled boots. Their straight hair reached to their elbows. They were the same height—five-nine. At a quick glance they could have been mistaken for sisters. But Sevgi's skin had a darker, more exotic hue. Her eyes were hazel while Cass's were green. It seemed odd to Cass that it was now in the midst of this madness that she noticed the resemblance. Once it had been another woman who had seemed her twin, even her soul mate.

Sevgi yelled again, but Cass didn't catch the words. She was busy recoiling as an ice chunk dropped near her right foot.

Frowning, Cass looked up. On the second floor, two kids in red and blue pajamas no more than three and six stuck their upper bodies out the window. An adult appeared. The kids vanished and the window was slammed shut causing a pile of snow to fall to the ground. It landed on a large cement flower pot holding a miniature pine tree lit in white lights. The horde around them continued to shout and brandish their fists. A woman in a flowing black robe and matching head gear with only her eyes showing withdrew a pair of scissors from her handbag and snipped the string of lights. Cass wondered if this was an act of defiance against the Christian belief or Western beliefs in general.

119

Inhaling a large gulp of cold air, Cass faced Sevgi who had just stopped talking to a young man and yelled, "What's this about?"

"Government corruption." Whop. Sevgi rammed against her. "Hey!" Cass glared at the back of another man who was already moving out of sight.

In the next second by the force of the human tidal wave, they were swept like debris down the street. Each surge was a struggle to remain afloat. Cass's heart raced as she battled to stand erect.

Only feet away, tripping over a deep hole near a gutter, Sevgi bent over and gasped, breathing heavily.

Cass sidestepped to make room for two other women in flowered headscarves and long polyester coats holding a placard in Turkish that she couldn't translate. A dark-haired man, waving a Turkish flag followed.

"There's over one hundred thousand on the streets. They're marching in every city. Look!" Sevgi pointed in the direction of the park where last week Cass had sat on a snow-dusted bench and fed the swans.

"Shit!" Cass said.

Armored tanks and water cannon trucks, looking like ominous invaders from Afghanistan, rumbled toward them. Suddenly Cass couldn't move. Nothing would make her feet step forward. She was immobile.

Sevgi, apparently understanding Cass's dilemma, grabbed her arm. "Come on, I'll get you out of here."

As Cass was dragged, pushed, and shoved, the tanks ground to a stop. Soldiers directed their rifles at the sky. Shots rang out. Cass locked eyes with a soldier who was aiming his rifle at the mob. The roar was deafening, terrifying.

Her body lifted from the pavement and then went down with a thud. Her breath had been knocked out of her, but she wasn't bleeding. At least, she didn't think so.

A young man to Cass's right threw a firebomb. Swiftly, he stepped in her direction, extended his hand and jerked her to her feet before disappearing into the ocean of people. Two men with handkerchiefs over their mouths lit and tossed snake-like strings of fireworks. Others threw stones. Hunkering down, Cass scanned the crowd. Sevgi was no longer in sight.

"Dammit, where are you?"

Fighting for balance, a powerful jet of water blasted the crowd and clouds of acrid tear gas covered everything. Taking the onslaught on the side, Cass moaned, coughed, and protected her eyes as she dropped to her knees.

Another shot ran out. Gasping, she clasped her chest.

A man with salt-and-pepper hair toppled over and lay beside her. A scar ran from his hairline to his eyebrow. A mustache covered his upper lip. In the madness of the moment, she was sure it was the carpet merchant she'd been avoiding confronting. Desperate, believing death was near, she reached for his shoulder. "I...I'm so..."

His eyes popped open and in the same instant she realized her mistake. It wasn't Umit.

Grateful that she might have another chance to ask for forgiveness, she helped the stranger to his feet. The man stared at her, backed away and ran.

"My God, I have to...I must...before..."

A rock struck Cass's forehead. Her world went black.

When Cass opened her eyes, she was lying in a deserted alley propped up against a bag of garbage. She stood, turned and stumbled out of the dark corridor.

She didn't stop until she arrived at her apartment. Safely inside, she began to pace, stopping to switch on the TV to the English-speaking channel. The entire screen was filled by an army tank. A soldier's machine gun fired in rapid succession. The camera scanned to two men lying on the street, focusing on a puddle of flowing blood. It returned to

121

the soldier who swiveled in another direction. Finally back at the blood. Then at the face of an elderly man in a skull cap. She turned away in disgust.

A scream made her look again at the screen. A man's leg stuck out from under the tank.

The newscaster announced that the march was caused by a car accident where a banker, a police academy chief, a member of parliament, and a man suspected of being a gangster were killed riding in the same car. False diplomatic passports, weapons, and incriminating documents were found in the trunk. The men were involved in a plan to build more unsafe housing in the Black Sea region. Photos of the dead occupants were shown. One was the bank manager Timur Sahin.

Her eyes widened.

"The people have had enough. They are marching to stand up for their rights." Pictures of more dead bodies filled the screen.

"My God, I could have been in that car!"

Horrified, she hit the Off button.

If Umit hadn't called, she would be dead too. He had saved her life.

She crossed the room and opened the door to the balcony. The street was empty, but she could hear the far-off rumble of people and the occasional sound of repeated gunfire.

An overpowering, all too familiar urge to run and hide almost knocked her down. She grabbed for a nearby table. After a few moments, Cass picked up her cell phone again and called the airlines. "I'd like to change my tic…"

Rubbing above her eyebrow, she glanced at the notepad on the nightstand that she had never paid attention to before. The words, "Pain won't kill you, but running from it might," were written across the top. She believed in signs and the words hit home.

Lowering herself onto the comforter, she clenched and unclenched her fingers.

25

Umit

The next morning Umit telephoned a reporter at the TV station.

By 9 a.m. one of the worst blizzards in Ankara's history hit the city, forcing the people on the streets to return temporarily to their homes or other indoor shelters. Mercifully, it lasted all day.

That evening, Umit lowered his head against the cold blast of air that struck him at every step and struggled to the shop. Ali's outer garments were slung over a chair. Umit, forgetting to relock the door, immediately turned on the TV in time for the evening news. Ali came out of the back room.

"At exactly nine o'clock each night, beginning with tonight, every person should protest by remaining in their homes and turning off their lights for one minute. By doing

124

this as one body, the government officials will know how we feel," announced the reporter.

"It will go down in Turkish history as "A Minute of Darkness for Enlightenment Protest" emphasized the newscaster.

"It will be a simple act, but give a powerful message. And now, for more breaking news…Tomorrow we will have an exclusive interview with the originator of this idea. A man who has decided to come out of hiding."

Startled, Ali glanced at his brother. Umit felt the look and raised his hand for continued silence. Ali returned his attention to the newscast.

Then in a loud, excited voice the newscaster broke through: "It has just been reported that one of the men in the car has definitely been connected with the mafia."

"Are you sure?" Ali asked.

Umit's mind went back to last night's prayers, to his readings, to his confession, to his screams, and to his wife's firm embrace. He thought about the story of Abraham and his test. It was strange how he hadn't thought of the story all these years. His father must have repeated it a thousand and one times. Abraham, too, had been commanded to sacrifice years of his life in prison. He had done so without protesting against Allah. Allah had been merciful and given him his life. How could he have been so weak to let fear of being imprisoned again control him? Fear was the tool of evil. He had failed that test. It was time for him to stand up like his new hero, Gandhi, and let the world know who he was and what he thought. He looked at his brother and spoke.

"It's time," he said, his jaw set. Then he added, "It was *our* doing, and not Allah's that caused this accident and the events afterward to happen. We must accept that."

Ali looked quickly at his brother. Their eyes locked.

"Let's play to quiet our nerves." Umit sat in front of the backgammon board and looked over Ali's shoulder. For an instant it seemed to him that his father was standing there,

125

about to speak. Umit cocked his head to listen: *Play well, my son.* The image was so real and the words so clear that Umit thought of asking Ali to turn around. He opened his mouth and then realized that his brother never saw the same things that he did. That was as it always had been and always would be. He said nothing.

The black cat jumped on the backgammon table, scattering the pieces. Fire snapped and spit in the potbellied stove.

26

Cass

Taking side streets to avoid the protesters and military presence, Cass made her way back to the swan park where she had met with Justina. It was a starless, moonless night. The reflection of a familiar figure appeared in a shop window. She quickened her step.

At the café, she took the same table she and Justina had shared. There were no swans in the pond. The branches of the trees drooped under the weight of last night's late snowfall. Bits of paper clung to low bushes. She moved her boot and slid a discarded bottle top across the brick. It snapped against a chair leg then shot under a shrub. Why had she suggested this as a meeting place with Justina? It was such a neglected spot. Cass had been so hopeful, so sure of herself. Now, like the absent swans, Justina was gone and by her own choosing.

Where did that leave Cass?

Standing, she slowly left the park and hailed a taxi, then shoved her gloved hands deep into her pockets.

All the way to Ulus she kept her eyes shut and stilled her thoughts.

She opened the door to the carpet shop carefully so the bell wouldn't jingle, then tiptoed toward the back room where she assumed Umit and Ali were playing backgammon. She would surprise them. Just as she had surprised herself by coming.

She hesitated. Umit and Ali were speaking in English.

"Do you think Cass Griffith knows that we are having her followed?" Ali asked.

Cass's hand moved toward her heart. She blanched and cut a glance to the front door. In less than ten steps she could be out of the shop.

"No, I wouldn't think so," Umit said.

"You think she'll ever confess?"

Cass leaned against the wall. The light bulb flickered. She looked at the door. He never needed to know she'd come.

"She doesn't have it in her," Umit said.

She slid down the wall, drew up her knees and held them close to her body.

The men continued to talk.

Cass gazed fixedly at the evil eye over the door that was so much like Justina's. Justina who had chosen death over life. Who Cass once believed had a soul attached to hers by a transparent, ethereal, delicate thread. Justina, her hero. Justina, who had died without Cass ever telling her what she had come to realize about herself.

And in that room sat a man with friends who were dervishes and women who admired him, a man who saved

128

her life.   But also a man who trusted her so little that he had her followed.

After what she had done? How could she blame him? If she faced him with the truth, could the bond that began to form in Diyarbakir strengthen?

"That woman is a runner. She'll be on the next flight back to the states. We'll never hear from her again. Your move."

Keeping the protective evil eye in sight, drawing her fingers into fists, Cass slid up the wall and with a steely resolve as her shield, turned and stepped into the room.

Outside, snowflakes swirled and whirled until with a whisper and a sigh they disappeared as the sound of an armored tank split the dark silence.

FLASH FICTION

Select a prompt, raise your pencil and see what happens. Then give the piece time to see what it's trying to say and revise to make it stronger. That's what flash fiction is all about for jd daniels.

When she was first encouraged by a colleague to write flash fiction to a prompt, she said she couldn't do such a thing. But loving a challenge and not believing in "never," she tried and was amazed how many stories and characters seemed to be lurking inside her ready to emerge.

The genre's key feature is extreme brevity.

The stories in this collection were previously published in the literary, online journal *Doorknobs & BodyPaint*. daniels holds first rights.

1

A Room of One's Own in Iran

A woman must have money and a room of her own if she is to write…

~ *Virginia Woolf*

All these years I'd made a living at my writing. "Tap the key with definition," my journalism prof had said. "There's magic in those keys. You can make a difference as a writer. Never forget: Truth has wings."

Shackled, pain encircling my ankles, I gazed at the gray brick towers on either side of the electric gate, at the barbed wire wrapped around a buzzing, sizzling fence. Glittering metal as far as I could see. I closed my eyes, but the brightness of the sun shining on metal did not go away.

Stripped searched. Photographed and finger-printed. Interrogated mercilessly. Taken to a dark cell where I would be quarantined for I knew not how long.

Stretching out on the cot in the cold, stone-walled room, I put my hands behind my head and stared at the water-stained ceiling.

Ah, Virginia, Virginia… Am I ready now?

2

Blue Hairs

"Did you hear?" Pepper asked.

"What?"

"Bert's got a new manager."

"Oh, that. So what? That ain't nothing to celebrate. Hell what's there to celebrate?   Hey, Janelle, bring me another beer, will you?"

Jake Goodall had places to go. Things to see. Oh, hell, who was he kiddin`? He'd lived in his mosquito infested hellhole since the twenties. Shit, it was 1951. He rubbed the back of his hand over his five-day old beard and glanced out at his skiff. Seas were too rough today. He'd hang right where he was.

"Hey, Jake, look, man, two more blue hairs just walked in." Pepper's voice was a sneer.

Jake rotated his head more to satisfy his friend than to look. Who cared about a blue hair? They all looked the same. He often joked about them spreading heavy loads of makeup over their wrinkled faces and turkey necks.

"My, oh my," he mumbled. "Now, that's something to celebrate!" His voice held awe as he gazed steadily at one of the blue hairs who had just walked in the door.

It had been a long time since he'd thought of a woman's beauty. After losing his wife when he was in his mid-fifties, he'd assumed he'd left that all behind—back there with dragging himself home on all fours and puking in alleyways.

He stood and for the first time in years straightened his collar and pushed his shirt down in his bulging pants.

3

Placa De Braus Monument

Courage is grace under pressure.
~ Ernest Hemingway

Gretchen, Hilda and Gil sat in the third row. Gretchen had not wanted to come to the bullfight. She'd been adamant. Hilda was neutral. Gil said if they didn't come with him, he would leave them at the border of Spain and go his way.

"Ohmigod," Gretchen said. "I can't look!"

"How could any man carrying a cape lined in pink be so cruel?" Hilda said.

Gretchen spread her fingers. Five young men half-circled the sword-wielding matador. One was the male version of Jamie. Damn. She pressed her fingers together and counted to ten.

The crowd roared their praise.

Gretchen opened her finger lock again. The bull was down on one knee. Two swords protruded from his massive head. She was a vegetarian, for Christ's sakes. She should never have come.

The man with the way-too-familiar looks swished his cape and took three swift steps backward.

She'd had enough. She stood.

"Hey, where're you going?" Gil asked, catching her by the sleeve of her sweater.

She pulled away. "I'm out of here."

"Hey, move along," a man behind them said.

Gretchen gave him a glare then inched sideways. "I'll be near the arch we entered."

As she hurried through the almost empty corridor, two dark-haired men walked by speaking Catalan. She leaned against the stone wall and waited. They stood nearby, chatting in an animated fashion. Not understanding them made her feel isolated, unwanted. How dumb of her. Why hadn't she bothered to learn the language? She'd always prided herself on how well she was prepared for a trip. She grimaced and turned her back.

Moments later, a horde of people streamed out of the arena. Gretchen heard Gil and Hilda before she saw them. "Hey. Over here!"

They waved.

Gretchen glanced toward the men who had made her feel so inadequate. One caught her gaze. She lowered her head. He strutted their way. "Come on, let's get out of here," she said, begging Hilda with her eyes to follow.

"What's the hurry?" Gil said. "Let's wait til the crowd thins out."

Hilda looked toward Gil.

Gretchen smelled hot breath on her neck. She turned and ran. Tears streamed down her cheeks. She knew why she'd left New England. She knew. Hilda knew. That bastard Jamie knew. Oh, how she knew.

She was a coward. A fool. A person who couldn't face confrontation.

The toe of Gretchen's shoe caught on a brick. She hesitated. Oh, how she missed her. She could be on a plane in the morning. On Sunday Jamie always stayed in bed reading the paper.

4

The Age of Reason

It is far harder to kill a phantom than a reality.
~ Virginia Woolf

It was impossible for her to spew forth banalities. Adeline Beebom was not that type of woman. She was a serious thinker—a person who demanded anything but the commonplace. Every word she spoke, every action she made was meant to teach, to enlighten, to empower. That she, as a governess, had little control of her personal life was a given.

"Miss Beebom, I must pee," little Reginald said.

Adeline's back bristled. "My dear, boy, that word is not proper." She raised her chin and sniffed her disapproval.

"Go ahead and close the door carefully behind you."

Turning toward the paned window, she gazed at the clear,

cloudless sky and the field of billowing snow. If only she could bring herself to go into that field and spread out, waving her arms and legs like an exotic, oriental fan.

A carriage approached. She stepped back and glanced at the calendar. December 15th, 1799. Yesterday the president had died. Today she wanted more than anything to live as she was meant to, but she feared she had given up that opportunity.

The door opened. Expecting to see Reginald, she looked over her shoulder, then gasped.

A woman in a white dress stood in the doorway. When she spoke her voice was a specter's whisper, "Adeline."

Adeline's heartbeat quickened.

The visitor nodded and extending her hand, beckoned.

Wide-eyed, Adeline intertwined her fingers and shivered.

5

Building Miami

Little Boy Jones stood at the stern of his fishing boat. Overalls tight against broad chest. Legs spread. White boots gleaming. "Get moving," he said. "Pronto."

Seventeen-year-old Charley Cooper would never get used to the threat of death that swam through the brackish waters of the glades.

Whirl of helicopter. Trees rustling. Birds shooting from limb to limb.

"Shit! Look at that boa," Charley said, holding a crate against his muscle-bound abs.

"Forget the boa," Little Boy snarled. "Quick. Get those other crates off that boat. And watch that mangrove root. It could take the side of your face off."

Little Boy's fishing buddy of ten years, Eddie, passed a crate to Charley who stacked it with the others. Frowning, Charley straightened it.

"Hey, we're not striving for perfection here. You hear that sound? That's the Feds. Get moving."

Charley's eyes rounded. "The Feds? But, I…" He looked at the crates, blanched, then stared wide-eyed at Little Boy.

"Don't give me that look. You knew what you were getting into. Get back at it. You think we would do this if we could make a damn livin' fishin'?"

Charlie's heart pounded. What had he done? His parents would have a shit fit. If he had a record, he could never get into the military. Eddie nudged him with another bag-filled box. "We're almost out of here," he whispered, applying pressure.

"Don't turn around," Little Boy said, "there's a `gator comin` our way."

6

No Inertia Here

"How're ya doing?"

"I'm up a few hundred. Fingers crossed."

Damon, the casino manager, gave the gambler a tap on the shoulder and moved on. The place was hopping this afternoon. He grabbed a glass of water from a passing tray, nodded to the waitress and sipped. His head throbbed.

On the way to work, his Beemer spun out of control on a patch of ice and twirled like a toy top. He'd been slammed so hard in the opposite direction, the weight of his body snapped the door open and he'd been thrown from the car. He rubbed his ass. No fun, that.

"Hey, Damon. Got time?" His new hire, Sondra Miller, didn't look like she'd had a hot time in the old town today either.

"Come back to the office."

He sat at his desk. She sat opposite. He knew she was

the type of woman who wasted no time with chit chat. He liked that. Time was money. Money was power.

"I'm going to come right out with it," she said. "I need a raise."

A raise? During the recession? She should be lucky to have a job. He looked aghast.

She wasn't having any. "Take a look out that window, mister." She leaned right. Her look forced him to lean left.

"Does the size of that crowd say you can't afford to give me a raise?"

Was this centrifugal force times two, or what?

"God, my ass hurts, Sondra."

Sondra grinned.

7

In Secret Kept

The human heart has hidden treasures,
in secret kept, in silence sealed.
                                  ~ Charlotte Bronte

Ira set down the beers and smiled with closed lips. I could tell his mind remained centered.

"Hey, Buddy, could you bring me another Corona?" The voice of the speaker was gruff, demanding.

Giving a brief blink, that would have been easy to miss if I didn't know Ira, he turned.

Placing his hand over his heart, he nodded. The gentle gesture was one of Tai Chi master to student or guru to disciple.

The customer flicked ashes into an empty bottle and

spoke in a low voice to her companion, "So, I told Gator to not gum up his life, but course he didn't listen. He headed for Texas and got involved with that crazy guy the feds got hold up, Karesh something or other.

"The Final Prophet. Mad man, if you ask me! Poor, Gator, he ain't never had no sense. Those floater, cult types are scary dudes. Stay clear of `em, I say."

With a gliding gait, Ira continued to the next table.

Sparkling lavender and azure salt water lapped against the dock's pilings. Two kayaks (one blue, one yellow) drifted toward the drawbridge. A dolphin rose and disappeared.

Torrents of swamp music bathed the room.

"How may I help you?" Ira asked. The question, like every word Ira spoke, was my invitation to a world where drums beat, incense burned and a steady hum calmed the universe.

8

Colonial Lanes

For most of history, Anonymous was a woman.
~Virginia Woolf

No establishment could indicate place more than Colonial Lanes Bowling Alley. Loud cracks from crash of powerful balls against pins. Whoops of triumph and defeat. Raucous laughter. Clink of amber bottle against bottle. Colonial Lanes was only one of the many places outside her bungalow where introverted Jessi Dayton felt overwhelmed.

"You're beautiful, Jessi. I love you, babe." Jack patted her hand.

"Oh, Jack!"

"Don't go all shy on me. You're a birthday angel." He

frowned. "Hell, it's 1940. I'm getting old, girl. Damn. But, you? Never."

Jessi adjusted the hem of her polka dot dress. Her? An angel? Hardly. Angels weren't baby machines. Already she'd had five kids.

Jack winked, and in quick succession gulped down four swallows of beer. He bent forward and coughed so long and loud, Jessi pounded him on the back.

"You okay, Jack?"

After one more hit, he straightened and shoved her hand away. "Damn it! Stop!" He scowled.

Jessi sensed a person's nearness. She looked up.

"Jack, honey, are you okay?" With a gentle action, the woman touched his cheek.

Jessi's lips thinned. Not again. She stood and headed for the lavatory. At the doorway, she tossed a glance over her shoulder. Jack was in a heated discussion with the pretty redhead.

Jessi closed her eyes, and as was her habit, counted to ten.

Doorknobs Winner
Doorknobs & BodyPaint, Issue 53, 2009

9

Laugh and the Whole World...

A bird doesn't sing because it has an answer,
it sings because it has a song
                                    ~ Maya Angelou

Sarah stands in the kitchen with Tom. He's wrapping the left-over chicken with Saran Wrap. His mood is gray—grayer than gray—close to black.

"You know what they call that in England?"

"That, what?"

She nods toward the box in his hand. "Film."

He pulls out another foot and tears it off. "Really?"

"Absolutely. So, instead of that being a length of Saran Wrap you're using, it's a length of film, funny huh?"

"Well, not funny hah, hah, but an interesting tidbit of

150

information."

Making someone laugh isn't as easy as it seems. She especially wants to make Tom laugh. A week ago, his uninsured house took a hit by Hurricane Andrew. The screen on the lanai was shredded. The roof over the master bedroom went. He lost a favorite palm and two orange trees. His also uninsured sailboat's scattered mast lay across a dock.

Laughter is a healing force. Everyone knows it. She decides to try again. Her eyes roam around the kitchen, landing on her book bag. Ah, hah! An idea.

She leans back against the counter. "Did I tell you what happened to me after class one night?"

He forces a grin. He obviously knows she's attempting to cheer him up. "No, what?" he says.

"Well, I couldn't find my car after class and the lot was full and this guy and woman in a car saw me looking and started shadowing me. Of course, that didn't help my concentration at all. I circle the lot twice. Finally, the guy gets bored and passes me. 'Having a blonde moment?' he calls out the window. 'I heard that,' I yell back."

Tom chuckles.

Sarah folds her arms over her chest and pouts. "You laughed harder after I spent eight hours basting our turkey in vanilla."

Tom roars and pulls her close.

10

Seat of Power

"It is, of course, unblendable, of an emulsion that displeases the eye."

"Yeah, I guess," Jennifer said, gazing at a woman in a kimono standing nearby under a cherry tree.

"All I was saying is that the city planners didn't do a great job of blending ancient Tokyo with the modern one."

Jennifer pulled at her mini-skirt and glanced at the toe of her high heels. Just as she thought, a speck of dust. She bent and flicked it off, then straightening gazed at a cluster of red, white and lavender petunias growing in the Hama Rikyu Gardens. "Isn't this totally awesome!" she said, wiping her brow.

He smiled at her, placing his hand on her right cheek.

"Why, Professor Reyda," she cooed, "If I didn't know better, I'd say you liked me."

He chuckled and pulled her close, running the fingers of

his free hand through his graying hair.

She pouted. It was a steamy, hot August day. Why hadn't they taken the trip on Spring Break when she'd wanted to? She settled on a bench that was shaded. She was a freshman at Cal State and instead of taking this trip then with her new lover she'd been forced to join a group of other freshmen in Cancun. How boring. Older men were so much more interesting. At least, that's what she'd thought until she'd gone to the internet café last night—alone.

Her cell phone buzzed. Smiling, she removed it from her Armani messenger bag as she walked out of earshot. "Hi, Mitsuo, I was wondering if you'd call," she said in a soft voice.

They chatted for a few seconds, then: "Do you want to meet tonight at a club near your hotel?"

She glanced at John. He was reading his travel guide. She memorized the address. After all, the professor was the same age as her dad. She'd restrained herself far too many times. She walked toward him.

"Your parents?" John asked.

"Yeah."

"They don't suspect anything, right?" His eye twitched.

"Hey, don't go all emo on me! Everything's fine."

"Let's take the train back. All this walking has me bushed."

After a quiet dinner in the hotel restaurant, John led her to the room. "Let's make it an early night," he said.

She was more than happy to agree.

At 11 p.m. Jennifer sat in the chair by the window watching John sleep. He was such a kind man, paying for this trip and all. She was so lucky. Twisting her right ankle, she slid her foot into her newest pair of heels he had given her, smiled and pushed off the chair.

11

Myopia

This one will be a Leo," Myrtle said, swiping her bangs off her sweaty forehead. Her newest just-hit-the-bookshelves buy, Orwell's *Animal Farm,* lay on the table near her elbow.

"Ah, you don't know shit! Last one, you was a month off," her husband mumbled.

Myrtle sniffed and patted her round belly. Picking up a flyswatter, she swung. "Got ya!" She flicked the dead fly onto the linoleum floor.

Edgar's face paled. "There ain't nothin` without right," he grumbled, gazing steadily at the insect.

"What you talkin` about? Without right? That don't make sense. You ain't made sense since returning from the war. Get a grip."

Edgar, eyeing the fly over his raised thick-fingered hand, spit a wad of tobacco into the black spittoon by the table leg.

"And don't tell me again not to kill flies. They carry germs!"

"Uh, huh." Edgar pulled more chew from his Red Man bag and fit it into his cheek. His gaze did not leave the bug.

"Okay, Mr. Wise Guy, fess up. What you tryin` to say?"

"What I was saying, Miss Smarty Pants, is all evil doings rights itself." Hunkering down, he scooped up the fly and placed it gently in the palm of his hand. His eyes filled with tears. "Just `cause you read, don't mean you know everything."

Myrtle guessed she knew enough. That baby she'd lost last year. What was the 'without right' in that? There weren't none.

Grabbing her stomach, she gasped.

12

Maid of Constant Sorrow

With long strides, Arly and Francis stroll toward the woods separating the family acreage from the neighbors. It's late May. It rained last night. They're heading for their secret spot to hunt morel mushrooms.

"The war sucks," Arly says, stuffing another paper bag into his pocket.

"War always is shitty." Francis slips his harmonica into his breast pocket.

"Yeah, but this one, well…You're lucky. You had polio."

"I hear Judy Collins just came out with an album."

"She's a goddess." Arly bends over and scoops up a barn cat. He pets it before putting it on the seat of an abandoned tractor.

"She's trying to attract more protesters with her songs."

"Oh, she'll succeed, all right."

"Pa says she has it all wrong."

"Pa's a Republican and a warmonger. He'd hate any anti-war activist."

"He thinks Kennedy is okay."

"Of course he does. He ogles pillbox hats on skinny women."

"He was real pissed when Tony got spit on. Jesus! He was wearing his purple heart. They said he was over there killing babies."

Arly frowns and hesitates. "Hey, what's that?"

"Sounds like crying."

They hurry forward and circle a gnarly maple.

"Hey, you! Get yourself home. Why are you setting there crying like a baby. You're no baby. You're twelve years old. Go on, get your little girl ass home!"

The teens give her a glare and continue on.

"Pillbox hats and white gloves. What a hoot!"

13

Equal Opportunity

"Hey! How are you doing?"

The wind caught his words and threw them up the face of the cliff. Sweat slipped out of the edge of his red and white bandana. Every muscle in his body quivered. His fingers ached. The toes of his rock-climbing shoes dug into the shale. His breathing came at the same rhythm as his heart. He would not fall. He simply would not fall.

God damn it! He turned his head to the right and looked up.

Lillian was high above his perch. Of course. She would be. She always was. Not that it bothered him. But, Jesus, what was he doing here projecting from a wall? Just get him to the top and he promised he'd never have a smoke again. What a joke. Of course he would smoke. Strike that. Just let me get to the top.

Good God! What was he doing? Asking a favor of God! He didn't believe in God or any other higher being, for Christ's sake. He was an atheist.

All those spiritualist types down there in Taos, he wasn't one of those.

So put up or shut up!

He stretched out his arm and caught another ledge.

Jesus God, would his collarbone hold?

It's okay women go higher than men. They need their chance. His fingers clasped a razor-sharp stone. Fuck! Blood oozed down his arm.

"Hey, Frank, come on up. It's a stunning view up here!"

"Shit. Women!"

A fly landed on his nose. He wanted more than anything to swat it. The fly moved down his nostrils, stopped and sandpapered his feet.

"Oh, please! Mother of God!"

"Frank!"

"Piss off," he mumbled.

He shook his head. The fly flew away. He sighed. It landed on his lower lip. Improvising, he curled his tongue and poked it out from the circle he made out of his lips. The fly disappeared.

"Whew!"

"Frank! Dr. Evans! Do you want me to pull you to the top?"

Frank grimaced. "Like hell!" He propelled from his right foot, clasped the next ledge and pulled, moving upward. "Ugh! Fuck!" he grunted.

14

Volcanic Peeks

Amber bends at the waist and gulps. "It's not like this hill is steep. I'm out of shape."

"Tell me about it," Kima says. "Wow! Look at those fairy chimneys. Talk about over the top otherworldly!"

As Amber straightens, a startled look flashes over her face. "I've been here before."

Kima grimaces. "You have not! This is our first time in Turkey."

"No. What I mean is…I've *been* here before."

Kima settles on a boulder. "You mean like in a past life?"

Smiling, Amber folds her lean body onto the rock beside her friend. "Yeah."

Kima sniffs. "I'd keep that to yourself, if I were you." She pulls out her travel book.

Amber chuckles. "You mean, like one's place in 1989

needs to be a rational place?"

"You don't want others to think you're ditsy, do you?"

"Do you really think I care what others think?" Kima closes her eyes, lifting her chin toward the azure sky.

Kima shrugs and begins to read out loud. "Many of the underground cities in the area were used by early Christians as hiding places before they became an accepted religion."

"I see myself wearing a long flowing gown."

"There's also lots of monasteries and churches carved in the volcanic, soft material."

"I'm walking among a group of people, reading to them."

"Let's see, red sandstone. Tuff-coned landscape."

"And, poof!" Amber snaps her fingers. "Like that, the woman of my dreams appears."

Behind them, a twig breaks.

15

Under the Hawthorne Tree

Mary Douglas holds a lace-trimmed hanky to her eye. "Those asters are superb."

"Yes," Virginia says. Her eyes are guarded.

"Virginia, I think Lillian would be pleased. Don't you?"

Virginia nods but does not answer. She lowers her head.

They stand under a fully leafed Hawthorne tree in the backyard of Virginia and her husband's Queen Anne cottage. A shovel rests against the tree. Behind them, an official from the county leans against the picket fence with his hands crossed. His Model T Ford is parked nearby. Virginia cannot see his eyes under the brim of his hat, but she feels his boredom and wishes that he didn't have to be present, but she knows he must.

The brick wall of the nearby, abandoned farmhouse seems forbidding and unforgiving this morning. If only Charles were home, but he is somewhere in the south selling cars for Henry Ford and can't be reached.

Mary, Virginia's sister, steps closer. "Virginia, you must cry. You must."

Virginia sighs, kneels and using her trowel, plants the cluster of pink flowers at the head of her child's grave. A small, wooden cross reads: Lillian Carlisle. Two days old. May She Rest in Peace. 1923. Her thirteen other children surround the grave.

As Virginia works, her wide-brimmed hat sweeps the loose earth. Dirt clings to the fingers of her only pair of black gloves. "Oh, dear," she says. "Oh." Her voice cracks.

16

Autumn Microburst

In one direction or another mankind strives
to live a supernatural life...
                    ~Henry David Thoreau

It struck Sasha Obreht that the hillside had the incline of a beginner's ski slope. It'd been a long time since she'd thought of skiing. As a bean counter who worked in a cubicle, she'd come to live her life in an orderly way. No chaos. No dust. Everything in its place.

Her pony-tailed son, Louis, walked around her SUV, carrying a drawing pad. "You're going to love this," he said. She wasn't so sure. "A cemetery?"

They were so different. He, the believer-in-the-otherworld. She, the what-you-see-is-what-you-get-parent.

Today she humored him. Spending time together was important. He'd be off to college soon. But visiting an isolated graveyard on a biting October day wasn't her idea of fun. Shopping. Playing tennis or bridge. Now, that was more like it.

Sasha took Louis's arm and they started up the hillside flanked by woods she had once played in as a child. That there was a cemetery nearby was news to her.

When they reached the top, Louis released her arm and pointed. "It's over there, at the end of the path."

Sasha reminded herself not to appear too bored. She stepped forward and was met by a surprise. "Why, it's surrounded by a wrought-iron fence."

"Cool, huh?" Louis opened the gate and stood back to allow her entrance.

She glanced at his sketchbook. "A rubbing?"

"Yeah, but come over here." He walked away. "Look at that," he said, swinging his arm wide.

Sasha weaved around several gravestones until she came to his side. She put her gloved hand on his arm. "Why, it's stunning."

Crystallized mist blanketed treetops, green fields and rooftops. Louis gave her arm a squeeze, then hunkered down and went to work.

Sasha placed her hands on the fence railing and let the cool breeze sweep her face. It had been too long since she'd been away from the city. She frowned. "Is that a train?" She knew it wasn't. She'd been raised on this farm. But still…iron wheels against iron tracks. So loud. She turned. Her grip on the railing tightened.

Louis's eyes furrowed. He dropped his pad and hurried to her side.

In that instant, snow eddied around the gravestone Louis had been rubbing. It swirled and whirled, flipping pages, mixing earth, fallen leaves and bits of twigs. In the nearby woods, no trees swayed. No half-leaved branches rustled.

165

Wide-eyed, Sasha looked at Louis. Louis looked at Sasha.

They smiled.

17

Way Cool, Man

He's positioned with his back to the three-story building, facing the carriage house. His slim butt nestles on an overturned bucket. Holding up a brass sash handle, he inspects its sheen, and then continues to polish. A cardinal flits low, almost brushing his head. He doesn't look up. A bee lands on his muscular bicep. He ignores it.

Hundreds of wooden doors and window frames lean against the trunk of a maple tree. A box of electrical wire rests near an open door. Copper pipes protrude from his truck bed stacked high with sheet rock. The rustle of leaves muffles a voice on NPR.

Alecia sits on the cement steps surrounded by coneflowers and hostas, holding an open envelope.

With an action of a loving mother to her new infant, he gently places the handle on a table made of two sawhorses and a rough plank of plywood. A leaf flutters from a tree and lands on the shimmering metal. Bending, he blows it to the ground, straightening the handle.

Quiet as a fly on a leaf, Alecia watches, her right heel tapping.

He picks up a board and carrying it to a table saw, positions it. Maneuvering a Tai Chi move, he guides it through the whirling blade. He holds up the piece of oak, glides his finger over the cut, nods, and settles it on another table, then picks up a second board.

Standing, she heads his way. He glances at her, turns off the saw and grins.

She takes a deep breath, and like a pelican in search of food, takes the plunge. "I've been offered a chance to teach on a ship for three months this summer."

"Whoa! Congrats."

"Will you come with me?" If he won't, and she's sure he won't, what will she do?

He cuts a glance to the building, lowers his head and shakes it. "How can I?"

When Alecia was married it wouldn't have occurred to her to give herself permission to accept such an offer while her husband stayed home. How could she be having such fun without him? In fact, she most likely would not have applied for the job. Or, if she had, and the acceptance came and she knew he couldn't join her, she would have torn up the letter and tossed it in a garbage can without showing it to her unsuspecting husband. The past pattern threatens to strangle her. She clamps her lower lip under a tooth.

"Yes, well…" It is so much easier not to be in any type of relationship.

"You'll go, of course. Why wouldn't you?"

The restored brass handle sparkles.

18

Dearest, I Am Going Mad Again

Every secret of a writer's soul…is written
large in his/her works
~ Virginia Woolf

Murky water laps against the narrow shoreline. Two shrubs flank a secluded opening to the sea.

Virginia stands by a hurricane-damaged tree tracing the aged, carved three-inch letter "V". Gently she runs her finger from top to bottom of the second "V". She closes her eyes and remembers the one-inch scar on her cheek, the curve of her narrow lips, her gentle, searching eyes.

No matter how hard she has tried, she has never been able to thrust out the memory.

"Virginia, I adore you."

Virginia's hand drifts to her heart.

She opens her moist eyes.

A steamer moves slowly toward St. Ives. A familiar figure gazes toward the shore.

Virginia steps forward, pulls off her straw hat and waves. The woman returns her greeting. Behind Virginia, a diary and pen rest on a wooden bench.

A cool wind wafts from the south and blows through her graying hair. She looks down. A tiny crab scurries across the sand, then disappears into a hole.

Virginia settles her hat on her head, strolls to the bench and opens the diary entitled *Summer 1925*.

Her pencil races across the page, faster and faster it moves until soon she no longer remembers the sea, the sky, St. Ives, the woman.

Moments later, she raises her face to the sun. Her wide eyes sparkle like miniature, effervescent jellyfish at dusk.

Doorknobs Winner
Doorknobs & Bodypaint, Issue 54, 2009

ABOUT THE AUTHOR

jd daniels holds a Doctor of Arts degree from Drake University with a dissertation of her poetry. Her award-winning fiction, non-fiction and poetry have appeared in various publications, including: *The Broad River Review, The Sylvan Echo, The Elkhorn Review, Doorknobs & BodyPaint An Anthology, The National PEN Woman's Online Magazine* and *riverbabble.* "Nancy's Woodcut" won Second Prize in a contest sponsored by Emerson College, Cambridge University in England. *Say Yes* topped the Best-Seller List in Iowa City, a UNESCO City of Literature. *Through Pelican Eyes* is the first of the Jessie Murphy Mystery Series. *The Old Wolf Lady: Wewewa Mepemoa* was awarded a grant from The Iowa Arts Council. The Iowa Arts and Poets & Writers Directories invited her inclusion. She is co-founder and an editor for *Prairie Wolf Press Review.*

She loves to spend time with family and friends laughing and sharing ideas and stories. If you have time, go to her Website and let her know what you think about her writing.

www.live-from-jd

OTHER BOOKS BY THE AUTHOR

FICTION

Through Pelican Eyes

NONFICTION

The Old Wolf Lady: A Biography
(First Edition)
The Old Wolf Lady: Wawewa Mepemoa
(Second Edition)

POETRY

Currents that Puncture: A Dissertation
Say Yes

Made in the USA
Charleston, SC
31 January 2015